IR

Also by Jabari Asim

NONFICTION

*Not Guilty: Twelve Black Men Speak
Out on the Law, Justice, and Life (editor)*

*The N Word: Who Can Say It,
Who Shouldn't, and Why*

*What Obama Means: For Our Culture,
Our Politics, Our Future*

*We Can't Breathe: On Black Lives,
White Lies, and the Art of Survival*

FICTION

A Taste of Honey: Stories

Only the Strong: An American Novel

CHILDREN'S

The Road to Freedom

Whose Toes Are Those?

Whose Knees Are These?

Daddy Goes to Work

Girl of Mine

Boy of Mine

Fifty Cents and a Dream

Preaching to the Chickens

*A Child's Introduction
to African American History*

My Baby Loves Christmas

My Baby Loves Halloween

My Baby Loves Valentine's Day

POETRY

Stop and Frisk: American Poems

Yonder

A Novel

Jabari
Asim

Simon & Schuster
New York   London   Toronto
Sydney   New Delhi

Simon & Schuster
1230 Avenue of the Americas
New York, NY 10020

First Simon & Schuster hardcover edition January 2022

For information about special discounts for bulk purchases, please contact Simon & Schuster Special Sales at 1-866-506-1949 or business@simonandschuster.com.

The Simon & Schuster Speakers Bureau can bring authors to your live event. For more information or to book an event, contact the Simon & Schuster Speakers Bureau at 1-866-248-3049 or visit our website at www.simonspeakers.com.

Interior design by Lewelin Polanco

Manufactured in the United States of America

1   3   5   7   9   10   8   6   4   2

Library of Congress Cataloging-in-Publication Data
Names: Asim, Jabari, 1962– author.
Title: Yonder : a novel / Jabari Asim.
Description: First Simon & Schuster hardcover edition. |
New York : Simon & Schuster, 2022.
Identifiers: LCCN 2021012780 (print) | LCCN 2021012781 (ebook) |
ISBN 9781982163167 (hardcover) | ISBN 9781982163174 (paperback) |
ISBN 9781982163181 (ebook)
Classification: LCC PS3601.S59 Y66 2022 (print) |
LCC PS3601.S59 (ebook) | DDC 813/.6--dc23
LC record available at https://lccn.loc.gov/2021012780
LC ebook record available at https://lccn.loc.gov/202101278

ISBN 978-1-9821-6316-7
ISBN 978-1-9821-6318-1 (ebook)

*To my parents, for showing me
the possibilities of love.*

To Liana, who embodies them.

"People won't believe you were ever a slave, Frederick, if you keep on in this way . . . ." "Better have a little of the plantation speech than not . . . it is not best that you seem to be learned."

—Frederick Douglass, *The Life and
Times of Frederick Douglass*

Got one mind for the boss to see,
Got another mind for what I know is me.

—Black folk song

Contents

Contents

All of us have two tongues.

The first is for them. A broken joke of language, it is a lament cloaked in deception, a bloody strangeness in our throats. It tastes of copper, salt, and dust.

The second is for us. It is a song of dreams and drums, whispered promises and incantations. We spoke it in the quarters, during the rare late nights and early mornings when they were not looking into our mouths for signs of betrayal. This tongue is rich, savory, and, if we're not mindful, can bring us to ruin. This tongue reminds us that, despite everything, we love.

I

The Gods Who Made Us

William

By my reckoning, I had fourteen harvests behind me when I saw the children. At the time, I was captive to a Thief named Norbrook, a tall, thin man with an unnerving stare and a smile that could easily be mistaken for a snarl. He was far from rich, with only a small farm and ten stolen people to his name. For our labors Norbrook gave us two daily meals of corn mush and bone soup, an annual gift of a pair of pants, dresses for women, long shirts for the children, a pair of ill-fitting boots, and as many stripes as our black skins could bear. We had hardships aplenty, yet we found some comfort in knowing that others in the world—rats, say, or snakes—had it even worse.

I was born into Norbrook's possession. Of my parents I had no knowledge. My earliest memories involve few human beings, Stolen or otherwise. Instead of recollections of first words or first steps or sweet lullabies that a mother might sing, I remember staggering with the others to the woods at dusk to fill our blankets with leaves. To assist and comfort Norbrook's pigs and cattle, we were obliged to pile foliage on the blankets—the same ragged cloth that sheltered us as we slept on the cold, damp earth at night—and drag them to the pens and stables, where we lined the animals' beds. This must have been one of my first tasks, tugging a weight nearly as heavy as myself, battling the swarms of black flies and mosquitoes as they landed heavily and pecked at my eyes, ears, and mouth. So often did I trudge and sweat in this manner that my young mind entertained few thoughts beyond this discomfort, and often I couldn't tell if I was dreaming or awake. Most of Norbrook's Stolen were acquired by schemes carried out in the shadows, including gambling, rigged auctions, and unseemly bargains. We suffered his tormenting while he wrestled with debt, claiming he would soon achieve a run of profit that would swell his purse and bring him the hurrahs and hand-clapping he so richly deserved.

While dodging his creditors, he learned about the ill luck of a trader named Bill Myers. This man attended auctions throughout the state, acquiring Stolen women whose days as breeders were running dry. Many of them had their youngest children in their arms. Myers stored his purchases and their babes in a shuttered log pen in town and assigned two old aunties to maintain them on broth and crumbs. Soon after, he gathered only the mothers and drove them south for sale, leaving their children behind, with an eye toward returning and harvesting them. But he was detained, and the young ones were left to suffer as winter approached. Once Norbrook learned of Myers's situation, he thought he might collect the orphans and fatten them up for a quick profit. He assigned me to prepare the wagon and go with him on the ride to town. But we got there too late.

Norbrook and I entered to the smell of rotting meat. Flies clotted the air with excited buzzing. Here and there lay lumps of flesh, which a closer look revealed as dead children. Some twenty in all, they had each come to rest with their backs against a wall, curled in shapes that recalled the wombs they had not so long ago departed. None of them was older than three harvests, hardly old enough to do much walking, let alone tall enough or strong enough to solve the barred door and summon help. Had no one heard them cry for their mothers? For milk? Perhaps the noise in the surrounding streets had muffled their desperate wailing.

Norbrook had arranged for a physician, a Dr. LeMaire, to meet us at the pen and give the children a looking over. Minutes after we got there, he pushed open the door, expanding the wedge of light our entrance had created. He reached in his vest pocket and pressed a handkerchief to his nose and mouth, shook his head, and muttered softly. I noted his watering eyes and could not decide if he was overcome with grief or driven to tears by the smell.

Just then, one child, sturdier and perhaps older than the rest, groaned piteously. Seconds before, Norbrook, frustrated, had raised his boot to kick the boy. Now he squatted and looked closely at the lone survivor while the doctor and I peered over his shoulder. The boy's ribs showed above his swollen belly. His eyes seemed sealed shut, although I could see some movement behind the lids. His nose and jaw bore the marks of a recent attack, probably by barn mice. Norbrook gently rolled the boy on his side, uncovering a clump of sores and a festering wound in his arm.

"Pity's sake," the doctor exclaimed.

A sour taste flooded my mouth. The boy groaned louder, as if in protest.

I had known that death could come at any time. You could keel over in the fields. You could be crushed under a wagon wheel, kicked by a horse, or have your skull split open because a slice of ham from a Thief's table had gone missing, breathing your last while the hound that stole the meat was still choking it down.

The deaths in the log pen, however, affected me in a way that no others had and raised questions about life beyond Norbrook's acres. Up to that time, I'd known nothing of the outside world beside the quiet town some ten miles from my home. I learned from the older Stolen that our Ancestors had been taken from a place called Africa, but I didn't know how far away it was or if the people there would welcome us back. Our captors, in control of our world and everything in it, told us stories to keep us fearful. They warned us that a creature named Swing Low often appeared in the night to take disobedient Stolen to a place called Canada, where they'd be punished and likely killed. The Canadians, they said, wore coats with woolen collars made from the scalps of the Stolen they had murdered. Even worse, they craved the meat of Stolen children. We were not in agreement about the truth of such claims. We questioned them as much as their talk of a divine savior, a man named Jesus. From what we could tell, they believed that he had once died so that all Thieves could live again in a world beyond this one, that they could steal and rape and injure again and again but only had to say they were sorry and it would all be forgiven. Their names would then appear on a list in the hands of a man named Peter, who lived on a cloud and guarded the gates to a place called heaven. It seemed such a silly story, a tale that adults would cast aside when they left childhood behind.

But we had our own strange notions, and they, too, required a willingness to believe. Our elders taught us that words were mighty enough to change our condition. They whispered seven words into the ears of every Stolen newborn before the child was given a name, seven words carefully chosen for that child alone. After the child learned them he was expected to recite them faithfully each morning and night. I had my doubts. Again and again words failed to save us. Still, as unsteady as they seemed, they were often all we had. Without words of our own we'd have no choice but to see the world as they saw it. And even though we witnessed life unfold through very different eyes, we shared with our captors a need to believe that names could affect the turn of events. We called them Thieves; they called themselves God's Children. We called ourselves Stolen; they called us niggas. Our language, our secret tongue, was our last defense.

Norbrook had sprinkled water on the boy's cracked, blistered lips and tried but failed to get him to sit up with his back against the wall. When Norbrook let him loose he collapsed to the ground like a sack of seeds. Norbrook spoke to the doctor without turning to face him.

"You think I could make anything off him? Stuff him with porridge, and grease him till he shines?"

"I'm reluctant to speculate," the doctor said. Although his hair was sparse, the silver strands reached almost to his collar. He ran his fingers through them, his jowls quivering as he spoke.

Norbrook nodded. "Not much to do, then."

"Might I suggest that you consider mercy, Mr. Norbrook?"

Norbrook squinted, still studying the boy. "When a horse's leg is busted, we show it mercy by shooting it in the head. Is that what you're advising?"

"Hardly, sir. I'm merely saying that with proper care this boy might fully recover. But it could take some time and no little expense."

"And even then you're not certain."

"No, sir, I am not."

Norbrook rubbed his chin. "Then look away. Both of you. Look away."

I could not. I felt that turning away would be a betrayal, that I would be failing the boy somehow. I watched as he blinked hard. Crust and phlegm oozed from his eyes, and he seemed to see us clearly for the first time. At that moment, Norbrook leaned forward and slit his throat. I staggered to the street, dazed and reeling.

The doctor was at my heels, calling after me. He could just as well have saved his voice, for whatever words he said were lost to me. I heard nothing, saw nothing as I lurched into the dusty lane, taking no heed of the pile of droppings I stumbled through as I made my way to the other side. A general store stood before me, and in front of it was a young boy, a Thief some six harvests younger than myself. In time I came to remember him as a skittish boy, well-dressed, with the satisfied air often found in those of his class. I would also recall that his boots gleamed and he smelled of flowers. At the moment I encountered him, however, I saw only the fear in his eyes, a look so disturbing that it shook me from my daze. At first I thought that my own dreadful expression had frightened the boy. But then I saw that he was looking over my shoulder, and I turned to spy a runaway horse, immense and wild-eyed, racing toward us. A strange silence continued to envelop me until the young Thief squealed. The sheer panic in his voice brought me back to the moment, and my mind awoke to the thundering of hooves. It was by chance that I stood between the boy and the horse. The troubled beast stopped mere inches before me. We were nearly nose-to-nose, its hot breath landing on my face like rude bursts of steam. Something had disturbed the horse as intensely as the scene in the log pen had stricken me; those forces carried us face-to-face, where our shared terror somehow ended in a sudden, eerie halt. I reached out with one hand and stroked the horse's trembling cheek. With the other I grasped hold of his halter. To those watching it seemed that, in an act of uncommon bravery, I had stared the enraged horse into surrender and thereby saved a young life. In truth I had done nothing of the sort.

There were more witnesses than I realized. A small crowd formed, last among them Norbrook. I suspected that he had lingered in the pen to collect one or more keepsakes—fingers, ears, or something worse. The most interested of my audience was Randolph "Cannonball" Greene, a wealthy planter. The others watched as he questioned me, Norbrook looking on from the edge of the gathering.

"Who are you, boy?"

"William," I said, keeping my eyes on the horse.

In a matter of minutes, the planter made an offer that Norbrook quickly accepted. He took his earnings to a nearby tavern, and I rode away in Greene's possession.

My new Thief was common-looking: skin pale as cream with

traces of crimson in both cheeks; a hard, jutting brow; a bold though narrow nose; and a slash-like mouth. When closed, the mouths of many Thieves were hard to spot if not for a hint of pink to mark their presence. When I was quite small, the old auntie who watched over me had convinced me that Thieves were in fact born without mouths. An opening, she swore, had to be created with the skillful use of a knife. She said it was a task that she had witnessed while attending several births, though she had never been called on to do it. Some people have suggested that the Stolen could seldom tell one Thief from another, that to us they all looked and smelled alike. That, I must say, is untrue. Our survival depended on figuring out their thoughts and remaining a step in advance whenever we could. Knowing the differences between them was a matter of life or death, and so we studied them with care, often committing their faces, gestures, and scents to memory.

For a brief spell I became Greene's pet. One astounding little nigga, he called me, although I stood as high as his shoulder and would soon surpass him. I received double rations until at last I became accustomed to Placid Hall, his home among his three farms. Having married well, he had easily assumed the life of a gentleman farmer. With his two neighboring plantations, Two Forks and Pleasant Grove, he controlled ten thousand acres. Placid Hall was his experimental farm, he called it, where he conducted studies of Stolen behavior. Seldom without his pocket watch and book of notes, he was bent upon producing a study so far-reaching and persuasive that his name would be known all over the world.

I have often wondered what force sent that horse galloping into my path. Though I place no stock in kindly Creators or magic words, I can't help but question how that simple beast found me and sent my life spinning in a new direction. Had it not encountered me in that dusty lane, I might never have met Greene. Had

I not labored under Greene's oppression, I likely would never have fallen for sweet Margaret and found Cato as a brother. But that was yet to come. At the time it was not the horse but the young ones we found in the pen who weighed heavily upon me, and there they would remain, those wretched children, for most of the ten years that followed.

Cato

I could say that my story begins at Mulberry Grove, the farm where I was born into bondage. I could say that it took a dramatic turn after I came to Placid Hall and became friends with William and the rest of our hearty band. I suppose both of those are true and would suffice in a pinch, but I'd rather say that my story begins in the pages of a book.

In most instances, the lady of the plantation was usually much more to be feared than the Thief who supposedly ran the place. Mrs. Adelaide, the mistress at Mulberry Grove, was almost kindly and therefore an exception. She took a liking to me because I was one of the few Stolen children among her husband's captives who didn't look like him. For a spell, whether out of tenderness or moved by spite for him, she began to secretly teach me my letters. From a book called *The Rules of Civility*, she read to me, taking my hand and tracing the words as she recited them. In this manner, I gathered the alphabet in my memory, as well as many of the rules. Not long after, her husband worked his way into her good graces again and she lost interest in our reading sessions. Angry at her for abandoning me, I tore two pages from the book and hid them in my pallet. On false errands to the far reaches of the plantation, I'd read them to myself until I no longer needed the yellowed sheets to guide me. One day the sound of our Thief's approaching horse startled me while I studied the pages in the trunk of a hollow tree. In a panic, I stuffed them into my mouth and swallowed them down.

When a man does all he can though it Succeeds not well, blame not him that did it.

Use no Reproachful Language against anyone; neither Curse nor Revile.

Labor to keep alive in your Breast that little Celestial Fire called Conscience.

In the years following my arrival at Placid Hall, I continued to recite the rules to calm myself, finding a comfort in the wonder and power of language that sustains me to this day. This fondness may at least partly explain my faith in my seven words. I said them without fail each morning, in addition to one more: *Iris*, the name of my beloved. Saying it was my promise to her that I would always reserve a place for her in my heart. Her name was still on my lips when I rose and left the cabin on the morning of the whispering ceremony.

It was just about sunrise. Two of my cabinmates, William and Milton, were already outside. The third, Little Zander, was last to wake but quickest to get going. He'd spring up like he'd been coiled to strike, only pretending to sleep. By the time he finished saying his seven, he was already wearing the grin that he kept on all day.

William was lean and alert, with muscles that rippled when he moved. He stretched and twisted to prepare them for a day of labor. Milton, a new father, had round cheeks, and eyebrows that seemed to dance whenever he was angry or amused. He looked hopeful but wary as he approached William.

"Good brother," he said to him, "are you going to give my baby girl a word? Preacher Ransom is coming tonight. I need one more."

Four women and three men were needed for a newborn girl's whispering ceremony. Milton knew that William would say no. We all knew. Still, Milton asked him anyway.

"You know I can't," William said.

"You mean you won't," Milton said. He looked at me. "I guess you'll be our seventh, then."

"Me?"

"No, not you, Cato. Who else could I be talking to? Swing Low?"

"Take care," I warned him.

"What do you mean?"

"The names you speak. You don't know who's listening."

"Are you talking about Swing Lo—"

"You know I am," I said.

In the quarters, the story of Swing Low was far different from the one Thieves were fond of telling. Our version told not of an avenging spirit who was out to kill us but of an angel who suddenly appeared in the middle of the night to free us from our captivity and lead us to friendlier climes. But that version was always recited softly, lest it land in the wrong ears.

"That's just conjure talk," Milton continued. "I believe in Swing Low like William believes in the Seven. And how much is that, William?"

"Not at all," William replied.

"All the same," I said. "Don't go saying that name around here. A still tongue makes a wise head."

I was glad that Milton's baiting of William had not turned into an argument about the usefulness of saying our seven, as it often did. I believed in them so much that I often pointed to them as proof of my certainty about a thing. "I swear it on my seven words," a favorite saying of mine, was an expression that would never fall from William's lips.

Milton continued to pressure me. "You can help my daughter get wise. We need a seventh tonight."

I shook my head. "You don't want me. Get someone else."

"What's wrong with you, Cato?"

"My voice is not fit to speak over a child. You know that. Get Little Zander."

"He's too young."

I understood Milton's urgency. A child who went unwhispered had no hope at all. Misfortune would stalk him all his days. That had been the problem with Cupid, the foreman of our crew. Nobody said seven over him after he was born. At least that's what the talk was.

If Cupid was worried about his luck, he didn't show it. His life at that point had brought him certain privileges, all in exchange for keeping the rest of us obedient. In addition to having his woman to sleep with every night, he had a rope bed instead of a straw pallet, and a wine gourd that Cannonball Greene gave him. On the morning of the whispering, he was the last to step outside. Tall and strong with a scowl to match, he had skin the color of toasted cornmeal. Freckles dusted the bridge of his nose like spatters of blood.

Nila staggered out after him, bearing fresh bites. Sharing her shame, we all turned away.

Cupid was the only man allowed to have a wife in the quarters. There were other women there, some in the big house, too, and more at Pleasant Grove and Two Forks, Cannonball Greene's other farms. Some of the men had mates at those places. But Greene didn't allow us to pair up at Placid Hall, said it distracted us from the work God made us for.

The Gods Who Made Us

After a quick washing in the cold dawn, Cupid made everybody pray. I usually just pretended to listen. I looked at the ground and kept my own prayer going, to distract Cupid's god. I figured—I knew—that any god who listened to the likes of him was a god to stay away from.

Too often Cupid's mischievous spirit made him look in my direction. He knew I didn't like to speak after he fought me and with his rough boot stomped my throat, ruining my voice.

"Cato, talk to God for us this morning. Say something. Put your heart behind it," he urged, opening and closing his fists as if he couldn't wait to hit someone.

I shut my eyes, thought of Iris. "Ancestors," I said. "Make us thankful."

It was bitterness in my mouth. But I meant every word.

Cupid put himself between the drinking gourds and us. "Niggas shouldn't be thirsty before doing a lick of work," he said.

That's when William walked up to him, got close to his face. Cupid had beaten every man in the quarters except him, whom he'd never even challenged. William had saved a young Thief from a runaway horse, and ever since then Greene had taken kindly to him—if you could call it that. Behind William's back, Cupid would tell us he spared him because he didn't want to bring Greene's anger down on himself.

But we all knew the real reason: Cupid was scared of him. Strong, fast, and tireless, William was never afraid.

"Niggas might not be thirsty," he said, "but I sure am."

He stepped past Cupid, dipped the gourd in the trough, and sipped slowly, like he was born a Thief in the big house instead of one of us. Like he had a whole day of leisure before him, munching pecans and sipping sweet tea on the veranda. If I were to note a change in the air at Placid Hall, a point in time when our story showed signs of becoming something thrilling and dangerous and entirely new, I would say it began at that moment. Cupid glared and spat but said not a word. I watched him watching William and it seemed clear that he would give up all he had just for a chance to do his rival in. Cupid turned and caught me looking. He rushed toward me, shaking his fist. I stepped back and gave him room.

"You one sad lump of nigga," he said. "Still lovesick over some wench who's dust by now. What? You got something to say? This is probably a piece of her right here." He picked up a clod of dirt and threw it at Nila. It struck her on the head, sending her down to one knee. She rubbed her temple and said nothing.

Neither did I. I had once responded to Cupid's teasing and paid a terrible price for my foolishness.

"You've been plowing the same row your whole life," Cupid went on. "Lots of places to sow a seed. But I guess it don't matter when you got a broken blade."

Still looking at me, he spoke to Nila. "Get up from there. Don't make me get after you so early. We got all day for that."

Behind him, William hung the gourd above the trough. He stared at Cupid's back without blinking, as if he could burn a hole in him just by looking.

Civility. Even now I marvel at the notion.

William

Cannonball Greene thought of himself as a thinker, a man of letters like the rebels who founded the country. In truth he was a man with too much money, too much land, and too much idle time. Twelve house servants waited on him and his family in the big house at Placid Hall, while another seventy worked on the surrounding lands. With so many Stolen people at his beck and call, he was able to devote long days to the study of Africans in America. Niggerology, he said, was an exact and demanding science.

The captives at Two Forks and Pleasant Grove were mostly field hands who tended his wheat, corn, and tobacco. His most skilled workers, confined to Placid Hall, included bricklayers, carpenters, tailors, seamstresses, and Silent Mary, a cook whose biscuits were the envy of the county. Their talents made Greene's household beautiful. They also made him money when he rented them out to neighboring planters.

Cato and I were trained as carpenters, and others in my company included Cupid and Milton, bricklayers both; Little Zander, a blacksmith's apprentice; and Double Sam, a handler of horses. We found ourselves banded together whenever Greene pulled us from our regular jobs and assigned us other chores. Certain qualities he claimed to identify in us led to our unhappy service in what he proudly called experiments. We knew from our work for other Thieves that they laughed at these projects and called them Cannonball's Follies.

Around the time that Milton's baby was born, the folly of the moment was an immense pit Greene had ordered dug into a fallow patch of land. It was about the size of a horse paddock and nearly ten feet deep. Stripped to the waist and coated with dust, we carted in granite brought all the way from Vermont. Using chutes we'd built ourselves, we slid boulders and stones into the pit. These surrounded a huge iron auger encircled by oak beams that extended from it like spokes on a wheel and from which we attached ourselves by means of ropes and leather straps. After maneuvering a boulder into the right spot, we positioned the auger above it and, by trudging in a circle, bored into the center of the stone. Others in our crew supported the work with pickaxes and hammers. As we ground big rocks into smaller rocks, Greene hovered and took notes.

We strained while Greene stared down at us, often pausing to instruct us to shift our bodies according to his precise designs. Occasionally he took respite with a cool drink and fresh biscuits brought by Pandora, a kitchen maid, on a silver tray. Silent Mary's biscuits were just one of many wonders known to come from her cookhouse. Greene had already studied her methods at length, recording every dollop of cream and turn of her spoon with the intent of publishing a recipe manual of regional dishes. There was a market for it, he was certain, and he'd even spoken of his plans for the resulting profits. Silent Mary, of course, would get none of those, save perhaps a new apron or a poultice for her ankles, swollen and sore from long hours standing before a hot stove. Even a full share of Greene's imagined bounty was not likely to comfort poor Mary. As a young woman of a mere sixteen harvests (or so it was reckoned; the exact year of her birth being, like all Stolen births, a mystery), Mary had been struck dumb when her newborn babe was snatched from her arms and hastily sold. She collapsed, pressing her face to the earth as if crushed by grief. There she remained a full day, rising only when forced to her feet—and said not one word from that point on. When nearly a year had passed without Mary speaking, her angry captor sold her to Greene. After many years of enjoying her food, Greene regarded her with an unlikely tenderness.

The racket we produced in the pit prevented us from singing or talking. With no other options, we sought escape from the drudgery by allowing our thoughts to wander. I could guess, for example, that Little Zander was thinking, as he often did, of angels and flying. Milton's head was full of worry about his daughter's whispering ceremony to be held later that night. My own thoughts alighted most often on Margaret, whom I had begun to love with a fierce devotion that surprised me. By then I knew as well as any Stolen that affection was a dangerous habit that would only bring more pain and suffering. While I trudged and the leather straps bore into my shoulders, I enjoyed a vision of her soothing my aches when we met again.

The last time, before leaving her cabin at Two Forks, I had taken each of her hands and enfolded them in mine. I held them firmly, never taking my eyes from hers.

"This is touch," I said.

I put one hand on the back of her head and gently nudged her face into my chest. With my other hand I grabbed a great handful of her hair and pressed it to my nose. I leaned over and whispered in her ear.

"This is smell."

I placed two fingers under her chin and lifted her lips to mine. She opened her mouth to me, and we kissed hungrily. After a long, wonderful, terrible moment, I pulled away.

"That's taste."

I placed her hand flat against my chest, spread her fingers over my heart.

"And this is longing," I said.

She wept then. Taking a kerchief from between her breasts, she used it to wipe her tears. Then she handed it to me.

"I'll never lose it," I promised, tying it about my neck.

She raised an eyebrow and turned her gaze lower, below my waist.

"Sure you don't want to tie it there?"

"You're a naughty girl," I said. "I just might have to swat your tail."

She grinned. "It's yours to swat."

Greene, had he been lurking outside the cabin with his book of notes, would not have believed what he heard. He was certain that Stolen knew nothing of romance.

"Billy Boy," he told me once, calling me by the nickname he used for me, "I say I love my horse, and if I've got liquor in me I might even swear it before a parson. But it's really just a kind of affection because we've shared some adventures. Your people, Billy Boy, you're full of sinew and rhythm, I'll grant you that. Bucks can tend crops all day in the hot sun, and so can the wenches. Your creator blessed you with strong backs. And the way all of you move to the fiddle—well, that could be more than rhythm. That might even be soul. With liquor in me, I might swear to that also. Bucks and wenches share adventures. But matters of the heart, well, I wouldn't squander much thought on it. Love, affection, those are concerns best left to those better equipped to handle them." He had hardly finished when his wife yelled from somewhere in the mansion, a high-pitched keening that nearly rattled the windows. The mistress was heard far more often than she was seen, and we all took it as a blessing. We called her Screech Owl on account of her shrill screaming day and night.

If I hadn't been stiff and exhausted, I might have chuckled at the memory of Greene's lecture as I labored in the pit. Instead I grabbed Margaret's kerchief from around my neck and held it to my nose. Then I resumed my pace before the others complained, and continued grinding stone.

For all our pains, the worst was at day's end, or whenever Greene tired of toying with us in that fashion. It was then that he lined us up and forced us to submit to a rude search.

"As if we had a mind to steal rocks," Milton would say later in the quarters, his bushy eyebrows rising and falling as we washed off the day's dust. We would scrub ourselves heartily then, and even Cupid would agree with his complaints.

In the meantime, we assembled and lowered our trousers, bending and squatting to Greene's commands. He inspected each of us carefully. I looked away when he lingered before me and tugged between my legs.

"Billy Boy, your sack seems heavy. What you saving it up for?"

"Nothin'. Suh."

"Make sure you sow your seed where it's needed."

I nodded.

"Margaret should be bigged soon, or I'll have to pair you with someone else."

"Yassuh."

I didn't want to be with anyone else. Nor did I want her bigged.

I liked to shuck her. Slide her shift up over her firm thighs, watch her goodness unfold like a sweet brown surprise.

But Margaret didn't care much for slow shucking, slow anything. In my recollection of those days, she never waits for me. When I enter her cabin, she's already naked and staring me down. She's more short than tall, the top of her head reaching almost to the middle of my chest, and halfway between lean and stout. Like most Stolen, she's been working since she could stand, tending babies, chopping weeds, hauling wood, boiling clothes. She's small but mighty. She jumps on me, back or front she doesn't care, just wants her legs wrapping around me and rubbing heat into my soul. We wrestle rough, down to the ground. I look into her bright eyes, surrounded by lashes so long they seem unreal. I savor her plump lips.

"How can a woman your size be so strong?"

"Stop talking. Do what you came here for."

The second time, same night, and she's on top.

"Shh," she says. "Just let me ride."

The third time, she wants it from behind.

I grip her hips in the dark while she rocks me. I feel certain I am going to die. I have never felt a happiness so real, so present.

Afterward I stand, stretch, and tell her I have a long walk ahead of me.

"No," she says, "*now* you talk."

It's those times when I tell her things I tell no one else. She listens as good as she loves.

Next day, I've had hoecakes, bone soup, greens. All that and I'm still tasting Margaret. Still feeling her breath on my neck.

Margaret

As my William has said to me more than once, a story depends on who's telling it, what they choose to mention, and what they leave out. There's also the way they tell it, and the way they tell it has been shaped by everything that's happened to them. They might tell it plain, like William, or with fancy words from books, like Cato or Pandora. My Ancestors' notion, that speaking of things can make them real, has stayed strong in me, so sometimes I've been partial to telling what I hope will be. William wouldn't let his mind set on those kinds of stories—about freedom and such—because he thought they were too unlikely to waste time thinking on them. He liked to say he was fonder of doing than talking, but I figured out that he did quite a bit of talking, except he did it inside. He'd run through possibilities in his head, decide on the right choice, and act on it. Everybody does that, I know, except William would do this without noticing that he hadn't included anyone else in his pondering. He'd just open his mouth and declare a thing, like, "We're going to go this way," or "We'll do this instead of that." When he said such things to other men, they usually nodded and obeyed. I did neither. I made him talk it out in the open air until his purpose was clear. Only then did I decide whether to follow or speak in favor of another way.

I don't mean to say that William's telling of things was always wrong. Sometimes he got it exactly right, like when he called me small but mighty. He used to call me that on nights he walked from Placid Hall to visit me in my cabin at Two Forks. I was partial to jumping into his arms before he could say a proper hello. Afterward I coaxed him into talking until it was time for him to leave.

I had been thinking of those nights when I nearly ran into Pandora while on an errand. At the time she was still personal servant to Screech Owl, who had left Placid Hall and was visiting overnight in the big house at Two Forks. Pandora was rushing to wash out her slop jar. She often walked around like she was in a fog of confusion, seeming to move through the world without taking notice of anything. Then she would surprise you by proving she'd been studying things all along. When I saw her, she spoke like she could tell what I was turning over in my mind.

"You all don't have much time," she said.

"What?"

"You and William. You all don't have much time. I heard Cannonball say six months have passed and Margaret isn't big. He said he might give y'all another six months but might not. Said he's going to give the matter some thought."

Greene had already warned us, so Pandora's words weren't a complete surprise. Still, they worried me, for William in his stubbornness had refused to do his part. He wouldn't finish inside me.

He'd love me to my satisfaction, and I'd do my best to bring him as much pleasure. But he preferred to withdraw and rub against me until he groaned and shook. I put up with this strangeness, even though I didn't like it.

"This world is wrong for babies," he'd say. "I don't want to be the cause of their suffering." Then he'd tell me again about what he'd seen in the log pen long ago, the flies, the young ones robbed of life.

"You had seen death before then," I told him, "and you've seen plenty after."

"It was different," he said.

"I feel a powerful sorrow for those babies," I said. "But they aren't ours."

He shook his head. "Of course they are."

In my nineteen harvests I'd seen as many dead babies as him, likely more. From September to October was the worst time for our youngest because their mothers had to leave them to go picking in the fields. Many of the women staggered back to the quarters only to find their young ones had breathed their last. The aunties who minded the infants did what they could, but too often it was not enough. The babies who managed by some miracle to survive the winter got sent out to the fields to work as human scarecrows as soon as they could walk. To me death was not the occasion it might have been in some other place. It was not something to get used to but something to expect, like hunger, loneliness, and the cruelty of Thieves. You could not let it shake you. Yet William allowed it to cling when I wanted to be the only thing in all of Nature that had a hold on him.

I first noticed him some three years after I came to Two Forks, when all the Stolen had gathered there to celebrate the harvest. I couldn't help seeing him as he stood with Milton, Cato, and the most agile of children, Little Zander. He seemed wide awake to me in a way I can hardly describe—thoughtful, quick, and alert. The hair atop his head was lush and curly, while he had almost none on his face except a thin ribbon above his full lips and a handful of coils springing from his chin. His skin was black and reminded me of liquid, like a rain puddle at dusk. I was certain that he was strong, and not just because of his tall, muscled figure. Somehow I knew that his strength came from the inside. Soon enough he saw me studying him, and he approached just as the dancing began. While the fiddlers fiddled, the foot-stompers stomped, and the bone-clappers click-click-clickety-clacked, we whirled and turned and skipped to the melodies they made. He was surprisingly nimble of foot for a man of his stature. And when the music stopped, there we stood, arm in arm. I didn't let him kiss me that night.

We worked from can't see to can't see. In between, Greene's Stolen traveled between his three farms, avoiding the paddy rollers to meet with lovers, parents, children. We called it night walking. William hadn't done much of it until he met me. But soon he was night walking to Two Forks to claim the kisses I had denied him earlier.

Cupid was a hateful, feared man, but he became a frightened little boy whenever he fell asleep. Every night on his rope bed he relived the horrors of his youth in his dreams, biting and slapping at Nila until she ended up on the floor. Rare was the morning when she joined the gathering in the quarters with no bruises from his fist and no fresh cuts from his teeth.

When he had about nine harvests behind him, Cupid belonged to a Thief named Mr. Reynolds. Another of Mr. Reynolds's captives, lost in thought about the woman he loved, let a piece of cherished crockery—a gift from Reynold's dear departed mother—slip through his hands. It fell to the floor and shattered into several pieces, broken without hope of repair.

"He had him tied up," Cupid recalled to Nila. "Made us all gather in the meat house. Laid him on the chopping block and cut off his hands and feet. 'Niggas were made to be broken,' he said. 'Dishes are not.'

"I was standing in front. Blood splashed my face, and I don't think it's ever come off. But I didn't dare turn away. Reynolds wanted us to look, and I didn't want to be next. When I sleep, I go back to that meat house. Only it's me on the chopping block. I try to chew through the ropes. I try to fight back. But no matter what I do, that meat ax keeps coming down. Something else that murdering Thief said: 'Lovesick niggas don't do nobody no good. Love will spoil a nigga for certain.'"

Cupid turned to Nila in the dim light of the cabin. "He was right," he said.

Nila wanted to go to the whispering for Milton's baby. But the others knew better than to invite her. Cupid would not allow it. He had no patience for prayers, only made his fellow Stolen talk to God in the morning because Cannonball Greene insisted upon it.

"It means nothing," he said to Nila. "Mumbling seven words or sitting and nodding to Preacher Ransom when he recites from the Book of Lies. It will hurt until it's all over. You know what people used to say about me? 'That boy got blood in his eyes. He ain't gon' never be no good.' But who among the Stolen hasn't felt the splash of blood on his face?"

Cupid chuckled. "That boy Zander is always speculating about the mysteries beyond Placid Hall," he said. "Asking questions of every poor fool who's wandered onto this place, every nigga awaiting the bidding of a visiting Thief. 'Tell me,' he says, 'what's over yonder?' He remembers what they tell him, says it over and over to himself, claims he's making a map in his mind. I haven't been but a day and a half from Greene's farms since they brought me here seven harvests ago. But I don't have to go anywhere to be certain that the land I sweat on is no different from any other. Nobody needs a map to know that there's nothing over yonder but more blood.

"There is no reward in tenderness, Nila. There are no gods and nothing to believe in but the burn of summer, the bite of winter, and the strength of my own two hands. Only fools would dare to ignore the truth of the world as it is. I'm no fool."

William

I knew Margaret was going to be at the whispering, but even the thought of seeing her wasn't enough to change my mind. If I held Milton's baby in my arms and looked down at her tiny face I was certain I would see that boy in the log pen, his eyes popping open just before Norbrook closed them for good. When I finally stretched out on my pallet, my muscles sore from grinding stone, I couldn't sleep. I got up and stepped outside. Cato and Milton had left for Two Forks. Everyone else was likely asleep except Little Zander, who wandered at night as often as I did.

Few stars floated in the April sky, and the farm was mostly quiet save the croak of crickets. I liked the night air, soft, warm, and absent the flies that plagued us throughout the long, hot days. Spring was well underway.

I wondered if Guinea Jack was awake. The oldest Stolen in the quarters, he lived by himself in a tiny hut some distance from the rest. Too old to work, he remained still most of the day, avoiding the heat. We all shared our food with him, and more than once he'd sent me to Silent Mary's cookhouse, a squat, smoky enclosure behind the main house, to fetch some treat she'd made. I was pleased for an excuse to sit for a while in his company, though we often argued and I usually lost. I didn't mind. More wisdom had slipped his memory than I could ever hope to gain.

He didn't believe in God. He believed in gods. He found no other way to explain the many different ways of seeing the world; how, for instance, some observers saw people where others saw mere things. How Thieves thought that they alone had souls inside them when it was clear that everyone—and everything—did. Although he knew more about whispering than anyone else—how and why our people began the ritual, why they chose seven words instead of three, say, or six—Guinea Jack's devotions depended on a pair of simple wooden carvings. They stood for all his Ancestors, he told me, and more. He called them Mother Root and Father Root. "When I bow to them, I honor all of Nature," he used to say.

He had come to expect my arrival on nights when I couldn't sleep. Otherwise I liked to visit him when the others were whispering over a newborn or convening with Preacher Ransom in the clearing, yelling and pounding the earth with sticks to get their god's attention. I told Guinea Jack that I didn't trust the preacher.

"He's not Stolen like the rest of us," I said. "He walks the earth a free man. I figure he struck some kind of bargain, gave somebody up. When we ask him how he got free all he says is it wasn't easy. I always feel like hitting him when he says that. And his flock. All that desperate wailing and stomping."

"Don't fault them for their desperation," Guinea Jack said at such times. "We're not dogs like some Thieves say we are. We're not mules, as others among them think. But desperate? We're desperate, for certain. You know that and they do too. Regard your fellow Stolen with mercy, not judgment."

"What about Cupid?"

"What about him?"

"I find myself thinking the world would be more merciful without him in it."

"That is what they want you to think. They made a mess of

him, and now you're saying you want to clean it up for them. Let them empty their own slop jars."

Guinea Jack seldom set foot outside his hut. When he did, he shuffled painfully and hunched over so far that he appeared to be looking for a lost object on the ground. Inside his hut, he moved well and was surprisingly tall. He had already set out two cups of brew and a crust of corn bread when I tapped at his door.

"Come in, come in," he said. "You're just in time. How are you, son?"

"Exhausted. Too tired to work, too tired to sleep. Some days I feel my bones growing old under my skin. I feel foolish saying that to you."

I took a sip of the brew. It was foul-smelling but deliciously sweet.

Guinea Jack chuckled. "I don't see why, unless you think I'm old. I'm not, and neither are you."

I sighed. "My bones think otherwise," I told him.

"The gods began the world in seven days," he said, "but everyone knows they didn't complete it. They left parts of it undone for people to build themselves. You understand? The world is never done; it is always becoming. See that leaf on that tree out there? It wasn't there yesterday. So that isn't the same tree. You're brand-new too. Every day."

"It's night," I said. "Too dark to see the leaves."

"Right. With my eyes it is sometimes hard to tell the difference."

"But you can tell the difference between brand-new and same old," I told him. "I was a Stolen yesterday. Woke up this morning and here I am. Still in hell."

"Hell is something Thieves made up, son. Careful or you'll take on all their foolishness. You don't belong to them unless you think this life is yours for all eternity. Part of you has been stolen, yes. But part of you is free as long as you can dream of something else. When you give that up, you're theirs, for true. Remember, son, we come from Strong."

"Strong," I repeated.

"Yes," he said, nodding. "There's no better word for the gods who made us."

Guinea Jack's brew was working on me. I felt my breath slowing, my muscles relaxing enough to make sleep possible. We finished our bread in easeful silence, the chirping crickets our only company. Finally I rose and told him good night but not before I asked my final question.

"Will this ever be over?"

"In time. When the Thieves find something else worth stealing."

"And then what?"

"They'll tell the Stolen that they dreamed it all up. That the worst things never happened."

Ransom

I proceeded with care on my way to Two Forks to attend the whispering. I knew all the trails leading there, those uncharted and those detailed on a map, and it was that very familiarity that influenced my caution. Those who stalked us as their prey paid little heed to the hour; the sun rose above gangs of kidnappers who grabbed free men and women off the street in broad daylight and sold them elsewhere to be consumed, digested, and excreted from the bowels of the republic. The sun's descent below the horizon brought bloodthirsty paddy rollers who hunted with an eagerness they seldom demonstrated in their pursuit of four-footed quarry. Worst of all were Thieves who had so little to do and so few prospects that torturing Stolen seemed to be their sole source of amusement. You might say that they were ruined by idleness. A Stolen child born in 1852 entered a world in which atrocities were commonplace. Whispering over her might have seemed faint protection, a parlor trick at best. Still, words were all that many of us had to offer, so we gathered faithfully to pour them into her innocent ears.

I had seen enough parlor tricks to determine the difference between words said to deceive and those offered in sincerity. My experience derived from my participation in a traveling medicine show in which Americans hungry for entertainment paid two cents for an up-close glimpse of the Wild Ethiopian Savage and a Hottentot princess—and, as a bonus, a chance to throw eggs at a nigga's head. I was that nigga. At seven I was sold to Luther Henry, an itinerant impresario and self-styled purveyor of diversions. For seven years I labored under his oppression. Depending on the size and philosophy of the town where we stopped, the audience could be as few as three or as large as several dozen. The Savage had approximately twenty harvests behind him, a simpleton whose supposed primitive fury consisted of hooting gibberish, slapping at himself, and pretending to make a fire. Whether he had been a lunatic since birth or developed his condition as a result of his privations I could not then say. Our impresario, bewitched by sensational tales of an earlier age featuring a poor woman called the Hottentot Venus, had acquired Isabel, a Stolen woman whose hips and nether regions were similarly formed, and displayed her with all the fanfare he could muster. Here and there he supplemented our company with other wretched souls whom he likewise exploited, but the three of us remained in his bondage as others came and went. Isabel's miseries were the worst of all we endured, not only because she was paraded before howling audiences in a state of nature—naked— but also because Henry allowed men willing to part with an extra penny to explore her more directly in the quiet of the night.

In time, circumstances allowed me to leave the medicine show and become what's known in some parts as an itinerant preacher. My travels as a circuit evangelist afforded me many satisfactory visits with the men and women at Cannonball Greene's three farms. I ministered at each place on one Sunday a month and counted many of Greene's Stolen as friends. William was not one of them.

I knew little about him, and he knew even less of me. He had no use for my message and little tolerance for such practices as whispering or the ring shouts we conducted in the clearing far from Greene's curious gaze. He kept his own counsel, at times disappearing into an old shack to contemplate who knows what. He usually found a reason to stride away with purpose when I appeared, bearing my cross and dispensing my homilies. Despite the distance between William and me, the other men's respect for him had not escaped my attention.

The planters in the region trusted me as a traveling preacher, a harmless nigga with a good heart and faith in the Word. I understood them more than they realized—and they relied more on the idea of me than the reality. Of the congregants at Placid Hall, the most charming was Zander, a boy of some fifteen or sixteen harvests. He endured the same travails as the others but somehow managed to do so without apparent suffering. His enthusiasm was expansive enough to encompass even a life in bondage. His confidence (yes, we can call it that) derived from his belief in angels.

The tales Stolen men and women handed down to their children included the adventures of Buba Yalis, or flying Africans. According to the stories, certain Stolen had been gifted with the power of flight. After chanting *Buba Yali* and other phrases now forgotten, they rose above their misery and flew back to our homeland. Others could do the same, the story went, if only they could remember the magic words. Zander took to those stories with all the fervor of a true believer.

One Sunday, he interrupted my homily to ask me about a particular passage in Isaiah. I opened my mouth to answer, but he stood and said, " 'Above it stood seraphim; each one had six wings: with twain he covered his face, with twain he covered his feet, and with twain he flew.' "

"You know the Word better than I realized," I told him. "I believe you're going to be a preacher."

"No, sir," he said. "I'm going to be an angel. Don't you see? Seraphim are Buba Yalis. They just called them something different in that place, but they're the same thing."

From that moment, Little Zander believed that he was himself a Buba Yali. Some at Placid Hall suspected he was right, for on his back he bore six circular indentations of unknown origin, in two evenly spaced vertical lines. They wondered, could the strange marks be the places from which his wings would sprout? The day was not far off, he promised the others, when he would take to the air.

I discussed the Book of Thieves under Greene's watchful eyes, being careful to never call it that. When he departed satisfied and left his Stolen to a few hours of rest, we retreated to the shelter of the woods. In a clearing, we began a ring shout by linking hands and marching counterclockwise, each step taking us back to a time before Thieves, before abduction and the routine infliction of wicked depravities. To a time before we were Stolen, when our ancestors walked with us and anything was possible. With the accompaniment of tapping sticks and the humming of sacred sounds, we raised our hands high.

"Brethren, sistren," I urged, "let us be who we are."

Their Book, that is, the Book of Thieves, suggests that the world will end in fire. Given what I experienced, it is not a notion I am inclined to scoff at. After seven years at Luther Henry's beck and call, the rush and fury of fire freed me from his control. We'd been turned away from a Stolen settlement, the name of which I shall not disclose. Suffice to say it was a place founded by former Stolen and hitherto unknown to me. Apparently Henry had been equally ignorant. The sight of unsmiling, independent Stolen, some of them armed, had driven him to seek refuge in the ruins of a stable several miles distant. There he drank himself into a deep slumber and collapsed atop Isabel in the bed of the wagon he used to transport us. He had chained the nameless Savage to a wheel and left him squatting on the ground. I alone was left unencumbered, as I had yet to give any reason for distrust. We were all asleep except the Savage, whose long practice of rubbing sticks together had finally ignited. The sparks he produced, having made contact with straw lining the wagon bed, produced a conflagration of ravenous ferocity. Waking quickly, I leaped to the ground and looked directly into his eyes. He looked entirely different, calm somehow; all traces of lunacy had vanished from his expression. His mouth, usually slack and oblivious to the ever-present flies, had formed a sly smile, his lips curved and tight with purpose. These he opened and uttered the first word I'd ever heard him speak.

"Run," he said. "Run."

I had seconds to obey him before flames devoured the entire conveyance.

I returned with haste to the Stolen settlement and came to maturity there under the kind tutelage of men and women who had known the whip and were dedicated to its defeat. They taught me valuable survival skills, talents I couldn't disclose to anyone beyond their borders, and made me aware of hidden allies to our cause. I emerged with a new identity, Truman Ransom, and the free papers of a dead Stolen in my pocket. In the interim, I had found my calling: to share news of the Promised Land with those prepared to hear it. To my immeasurable dissatisfaction, nearly two decades on the road had uncovered fewer of them than I had hoped.

Cato

The last time I saw Iris she was bound to the back of a cart, her wrists tied in front of her. Another rope was wrapped around her neck. Her new Thief had shucked her carelessly. One breast out in the light, the other covered. Her lips were bruised, cracked, and dry. At first it seemed as if she didn't see me. Then she licked her lips.

"Cato," she said. She didn't sound like herself. Her voice was hollow and far away, as if she were trapped in the bottom of a deep well.

"Best forget about Iris," Cannonball Greene had told me. "It can't be helped. My visitor has become attached to her."

Attached. That's why I had not seen her for several long days.

"He told me he has to have her. I told him it would require more than he was prepared to pay. I quoted him a high figure, and still he would not relent. Don't go feeling sorry for yourself, Cato. That would just slow you down, and I need you to work. I will not have you slacking in your duties."

I ran to Two Forks. I knew there would be consequences, but I didn't care. Swearing on my seven words that I could endure any punishment, I ran until I found her tied to that cart. I moved to touch her, but a Thief, Greene's visitor, appeared beside her, raising a firearm. He pointed it at me while stroking her hair with his other hand. She flinched, and he yanked her closer.

"Take another step, nigga, and I will shoot you where you stand."

"Cato," she said. "Don't."

"But you're mine," I reminded her.

"Hardly," the Thief said. "I got a paper here that says she's bought and paid for."

"I have to touch you, Iris. Please, suh, I have to touch her. Just this once."

"Do so and die."

I stood in place while he aimed his gun at me. Finally, satisfied that I would obey, he loaded Iris into the bed of his cart and drove away. Even as they faded from my view, I convinced myself that this great injustice would be noticed, that fate would not let it stand. Somehow, some way, my Iris would be returned to my embrace.

A few miles down the road, the cart threw an axle. Iris was flung to the ground, never to rise again. Greene declined to compensate his visitor for his loss.

"My condolences," he told him, "but a deal is a deal."

I avoided my reflection afterward. I learned to wash myself in the stream while staring up at the sky. I could carry a pail without looking on the surface of the water it contained. I couldn't stand seeing myself without Iris beside me.

I resolved to die. When that proved futile, I joined the ranks of the sullen. My condition was not uncommon among men and women in our predicament. We moved as if lost in dreams; we ate without tasting, slept without resting, listened without hearing. Others avoided us for fear of catching our ailment because they knew that not caring meant not living, and they had chosen to live. I would have remained among that disconsolate company if not for Cupid.

During a rare respite on a late Saturday, he taunted me in the quarters. I had learned to pay little heed to his teasing, but on that day, he managed to catch my attention by exposing the memory of Iris to his ridicule. He boasted of his familiarity with her, an intimacy that until that moment had been unknown to me.

"That's right, I had her," he said. "The night I whipped that nigga Big Ned and won Cannonball a heap of money. Know what he gave me? A taste of his good scotch. I'm the only nigga you know who's had scotch. And he gave me my choice. 'Winner's choice,' he said. I said I'd take Iris. She didn't want to, but I didn't care. It was fair to middling. The meat was a little tough, but I made it do."

"What did you say?" I advanced on him, nearly delirious. He seemed delighted.

"I said I had your wench."

I swung at him, missing by a great deal and nearly hurling myself to the ground. I bellowed, and he bellowed back, mocking me. We circled each other. He chuckled and connected solidly with my nose, my eye. Everywhere I turned, his fist was waiting. It landed against my jaw, filling my mouth with blood. I tottered, then fell to the earth on my hands and knees. I pressed against the ground and tried to rise. Through my one good eye I saw Milton gesturing with his hands, urging me to stay down. I took his advice and rolled over onto my back. I had hardly stopped moving when I looked up and saw Cupid's boot hovering above my throat. I blinked and it was still there. Then it came down.

Everything was white. Whiteness covering my eyes and nose like a caul, sealing my lips. I struggled against it, fighting for breath, then I woke to the sound of Screech Owl shrieking somewhere in the main house. Above me, the fading sun streamed through the clouds and birds sang sweetly, unaware of my suffering. I struggled to my feet and stumbled to my cabin, where I fell into a long, dreamless slumber. When I woke and tried to speak, my voice had been trampled to a husky croak.

The beating I received at Cupid's hands was nothing compared to the hole left in me by Iris's absence. Her tender affection had led me to take leave of my senses, to believe myself an exception to the belief that all Thieves seemed to share, that people like me could know nothing of love.

I knew that I was not the first Stolen to have his heart broken. I had seen it firsthand while still at Mulberry Grove. I tended crops as a young boy, rising with the other field hands at the sound of the driver man's horn. We stumbled from our cabins, yawning in the dark until a pine knot was set ablaze.

One couple, Isaac and Oney, were always last to wake. After several long minutes the two of them would emerge stretching and grinning, their faces aglow in the orange light. One of the old hands would look at the pair and cluck his tongue.

"It's a wonder that shack is still standing," he'd say. "Likely them two have worn a rut in the ground."

Isaac and Oney used to love so loud that everybody grumbled. Folks were amazed that they could get up and toil after all that tussling and giggling. Seemed like they didn't sleep at all, and yet they rose up smiling.

All through the day, Isaac kept his eyes on Oney. Whether he was tending tobacco or mending a fence. Whether Oney was right in front of him or far afield. The other men once bet him he couldn't go more than a dozen words without mentioning her name. He lost, laughing.

The Thief of Mulberry Grove suddenly sold Oney to a farm ten miles away. Ten miles between Isaac and his beloved was no distance at all to him. He'd sneak out of our quarters after dark and return before the horn sounded, until he was caught. Our Thief thought Isaac had been plotting with others to steal away to freedom. When he learned that Isaac was stealing away to Oney, he had him pickled and threatened him with death.

"You dumb wretch," our Thief said. "All these wenches round here and you want to die for the one I say you can't have?"

"If it takes dyin'," Isaac told him.

I knew how he felt. I wanted to belong to Iris when I didn't even belong to myself. In the eyes of the world I was not a self but a thing. My story was not my own. Like the rules I had stashed away as a youth, my existence was confined to a few pages torn from someone else's book.

Just when I thought I'd become accustomed to the loneliness of a life without Iris, I found Pandora. Working in the main house, she had somehow vexed Screech Owl and got sent to sweat in the kitchen with Silent Mary. She looked at everything and everyone as a surprise. She was always slow to answer, as if struggling with a dream she couldn't shake loose. Pandora, pretty with thick braids and golden skin, was nearly as tall as my Iris. I tried not to look at her. I had sworn on my seven words that my body was done with women, and she was much too young besides. Still, I couldn't help being aware of her presence when she appeared at the pit, bearing a light repast for Cannonball Greene on a silver tray.

I looked up and saw her standing so still, the silver tray steady in her hands. Her face betrayed no expression, and she seemed as solid and heavy as the stones surrounding us. I could not help but wonder at her thoughts.

Pandora

Before my friendship with Margaret, I'd seen women like her mostly from a distance. Barely clad in rags and castoffs, they were often confined to the quarters and the fields where they hacked and pulled and planted. Although I seldom interacted with them, I knew they went to their night's rest with bruised backs and woke up with knotted muscles and jaws aching from clenching their teeth through the night. I knew all this without laboring beside them because I had been forced to perform burdensome obligations of my own and I often arose in the morning suffering the same afflictions. My brief conversations with them made clear that they often regarded me and other house Stolen as creatures of strange privilege, with simple tasks that caused us little heartache or agony. For my part, I often thought they were the ones who had it easy, that no part of life in the quarters could equal the punishments I endured. I was wrong, of course, and so were they. All our tasks were onerous.

Among my duties at Placid Hall, standing above the pit beside Cannonball Greene was a far better plight than being left alone with Screech Owl.

She used to wait until her slop jar was full before making me carry it outside and stand in the yard. Watching from the open upstairs window, she ordered me to hold the vessel above my head until my arms bent under the strain. Finally, when my limbs began to shake violently, she made me tip the contents upon myself. I sometimes had to stand there for hours as the day grew hotter, baking in Screech Owl's waste. She thought that the spectacle of me soiled and stinking would discourage her husband's appetites, but, if anything, it only made him crave me more. He knew his wife's perversities would regularly send me dashing to the stream for urgent cleansing. Finding some business nearby, he'd fasten his eyes on me while I scrubbed and rinsed. We all—men and women both—had been naked before him countless times, forced to disrobe on the flimsiest of pretenses. The women in his fields, for example, had to strip and hand over their ragged dresses at the end of the harvest, when Greene presented them with the dress they'd wear during the following year. He made a great show of having them try on their new outfits, though they had no other options and the dresses—little more than burlap sacks with holes for sleeves—hardly varied in size or quality. Thus accustomed, bathing brought me so much pleasure that not even his lustful staring could diminish my delight. I always lingered in the stream as long as I dared, away from the main house and away from Screech Owl, who placed her faith in powders and behaved as if soap and water were devils' instruments. After I dried and returned to the house, Greene seldom dared to do more than squeeze and caress, so fearful was he of Screech Owl's wrath, and yet I felt that in his heart he nurtured more intimate designs. I convinced myself that I could survive his advances if I regarded him as a household pest, like the flies and mosquitoes that never left us alone.

I had few friends. Many of the other Stolen women held me in contempt, thinking that my mixed blood meant divided loyalties. The men, misunderstanding my relations with Greene, were inclined to look upon me as damaged goods. I found some comfort in the company of Silent Mary, whose melancholy nature suited me. Though Mary did not speak, she had learned to endow her gestures with great meaning. Every raised eyebrow and curled lip conveyed precise instructions, from *Take care with the salt* to *Add more wood to the fire*. Planters from farms throughout the county sent their Stolen cooks to study and practice under her knowing gaze. Watching her preside over her smoky cookhouse was akin to watching an elaborate dance. The Thieves, with their reels and waltzes, couldn't begin to match the majestic grace of Silent Mary and her helpers as they moved about her tiny space, conjuring tasty confections from the smoke and flames.

I came to know Mary a good deal more when Screech Owl banished me from her chambers. Thereafter I divided my time between standing above the pit; laboring in the cookhouse, where I assisted Silent Mary; and toiling at the laundry station, where Nila and I washed the family's linens. Didn't that pitiful woman know that those places belonged to Cannonball Greene as much as the main house did, that there was no place she could hide me?

During the many afternoons I stared down into the pit while Greene gave orders and took notes, all but one of the men grinding stone avoided looking at me. In addition to the danger and sheer misery of their labors, each, I could see, had particular habits and concerns. Cupid's violent temper was obvious to all, for example, and Milton nearly trembled with excitement, his mind filled with thoughts of his newborn child. Double Sam, whose prowess with horses was known beyond the estate, kept his head cocked to the side, talking ceaselessly to his invisible companion. William was stolid and determined when not distracted by thoughts of Margaret, and Little Zander regarded the strange operation as a process designed to help him become strong enough to take flight. Of all the men, Cato intrigued me most. Unlike the others, he managed to sneak a glance in my direction with each rotation. He was older than I, that much was easy to tell. He had a full head of hair and an even more abundant beard, both of them streaked with gray.

His skin was a lovely shade of dark brown, but it, too, showed signs of wear. Still, I liked the look of him as he lifted rocks, inspected them, and fed them again into the great wheel. I sensed that anything—anyone—that landed in his hands would be gently cradled and treated with care.

Cato

Because the crescent moon refused to linger for long behind the black and gray clouds that ambled past it, we stuck mostly to the woods. Here and there, enough shadows obscured the roads to enable us to briefly leave the canopied white oaks, hickories, sweet gums, yellow poplars, and loblollies for the path worn smooth by horsemen and wagon wheels. In this manner, Milton and I made our way from Placid Hall to Two Forks, leaping from the road just before the approach of two paddy rollers, whom we knew as Tanner and Kirk. They rode right by us, dragging a Stolen man behind their mounts. He was naked to the waist. The moon's light revealed fresh, red streaks glistening along the length of his back. He moved at a forced trot despite his weariness, lest his slackening pace draw him into the horses' hooves. His captors appeared to ignore his struggles.

I asked Milton if he knew him.

"I might," Milton said, "but I can't tell with his face so swollen."

"May the Ancestors help him," I said.

We met in the largest cabin, made ready for our arrival. There we found Margaret; Milton's woman, Sarah, holding their infant; and a pair of Two Forks women whom I did not know. Ransom, as was expected, had arrived earlier. He greeted us while Milton went straight to his family and hugged them fiercely. They remained thus embraced until Ransom cleared his throat. Even then they could not part easily.

After a moment I asked Ransom how he missed Tanner and Kirk along the way. "They were out for blood tonight," I said.

"Same as any night," Margaret said.

"The question, friend," Ransom said, "is how did *they* miss *me*? I credit my good fortune to the Ancestors. I'm grateful for their timely intervention."

"Nice words," I croaked. "But, respectfully, they do not answer the question. Is there a hiding place along this way that you have not disclosed? Knowing of its existence would surely help us all. How did you manage to elude them?"

"It wasn't easy" was all he said.

I knew few of the requirements of whispering beyond my part in the ritual, from which I had been absent since my ordeal under Cupid's boot. During his Sunday visits to Greene's three farms, Preacher Ransom made sure that certain members of his flock learned every gesture and incantation of the ceremony. "We must not allow the old ways to die when I do," he often said. In contrast to those sunlit days when Ransom preached, his presence at whisperings was pursued without the approval of Thieves and therefore conducted under cover of darkness.

Beneath the light of a few flickering pine knots, Sarah dipped the baby into a pan of water. Even in the dimness I could detect signs of only one parent in the girl's countenance. The twinkle in her eyes came from Sarah, as did her mouth, framed by dimples. Knowing little of Sarah's tendencies, I couldn't speculate regarding the affect they would have on the infant. But I knew enough of Milton's to wonder which of his qualities the baby would inherit. He was trained as a bricklayer, but his real talent was making pictures. Those of us who'd seen his creations could proclaim with confidence that the Ancestors guided his right hand.

With just a pointed stick and a patch of dust, Milton stirred marvels to life. He drew stars whirling in the night's infinite blackness, great cities of his imagination, signs and wonders he'd seen in dreams. He drew faces too. We could describe a Stolen long lost to this life and he'd make her rise from the ground, seemingly as real as if she were drawing breath. In the days leading up to the birth, he drew his daughter's face again and again. Her arrival only proved the strength of his abilities. Every detail had been exact, right down to the small mole on her downy cheek. Milton's pictures were one of our cherished secrets, fussed over and fondly remembered after the wind and rain had washed them away. The world beyond us knew nothing of his gift.

The baby, bathed and rubbed down with warm oil, was wrapped in swaddling clothes. Preacher Ransom held her and spoke in tongues, mumbling ancient phrases while we hummed softly. Once finished, he passed the baby to Sarah. She gathered her in her arms. Moving in a circle, each of us paused when we reached the quietly squirming infant. One by one, we whispered.

A baby fortunate to survive long enough to acquire the gift of speech learned quickly about the world into which she was born. There was the likelihood she would never have a chance to use such words as *mother* or *father*. Instead she would learn terms like *Stolen* and *Thief* right after she learned her own name. But no matter the circumstances, she would always find sustenance in the seven words whispered in her ear. They were our constant companions through every tribulation and every brief moment of transcendence. They reminded us to breathe in the morning and be grateful for air. For adults to think of their own seven words while taking part in a whispering was not unusual. Quite naturally, my words came to mind and I saw them as vividly as phrases printed in the pages of the *Rules of Civility. Stay. Think. Hold. Fancy. Endure. Give. Light.*

But they quickly gave way to the words Greene said to me when I learned that my Iris had been sold away, carted off only to die in an accident just miles from the spot where I last saw her. His advice, that it would be best to think no more of her, had seemed cold and unfeeling. I suddenly perceived that it nonetheless possessed the virtue of being true. I arrived at Sarah's shoulder and put my lips next to the baby's ear. I tried to speak as softly, as gently as I could.

"Forget," I whispered.

William

A fortnight after the whispering, Milton drew two squares on the ground. Each of them was long enough and wide enough for a full-grown man to lie down and stretch out his arms. He squatted on the ground beside the first while Little Zander stood near him and watched. I was at the trough, washing my supper plate and pondering a visit with Guinea Jack. Cato relaxed at the entrance of our cabin, looking on from a distance.

Taking up his pointed stick, Milton drew the stars as they looked overhead that night. None of us knew the names, but a glance at the sky proved that he had copied them faithfully.

Milton's art was all the more remarkable because he had favored his left hand as a child. During one of our nighttime journeys to Two Forks, he told me how his preference switched from one hand to the other.

"Did you know your mother, William?"

I told him I didn't.

"Neither did I. But I did know my grandmother. I had her beside me my first thirteen harvests. A grandmother is a wonderful thing. One summer day, not long after my grandmother joined the Ancestors, I fell from a tree and hurt my hand. My fingers were broken and bent. An auntie straightened them as best she could and put healing balm on them. Then she wrapped them in cloth. They got better, but it took some time, and they still trouble me in bad weather. As you can see, they aren't all the way straight."

I'd noticed his fingers but hadn't been curious about them. Gashes, bruises, dents, and the like marked all our skins. In all my days I had never encountered a Stolen whose back was not scarred.

"When the auntie was tending to me, I screamed. I felt ashamed to be so weak," Milton went on. "However, in the midst of my pain my Ancestors gave me the notion to dream. So I did. I put myself on my grandmother's lap. I had a splinter in my finger, and she was taking it out. She sang to me, comforted me, helped me through my hurt. Some days I can't remember my grandmother anymore, how she looked or smelled—and I become uncertain whether I even knew her at all. But I know it was her song. I sang it truly, loudly, and with deep feeling. She got me through."

The drawing had been Zander's idea. He called it a star map.

"I'll need to know more about the heavenly bodies so that I can steer by them," he explained. "When I take to flying, I don't want to get lost up there and come down in the wrong place."

Cato and I moved to get a closer look. Cupid staggered out of his cabin stinking of wine. He watched for a while, then spat, just missing Little Zander. "The stars are no use to us," he said.

"Watch what seeds you plant in that boy's head," he warned Milton. "Don't know what fruit they'll yield." He belched and sauntered back to his cabin.

Milton filled the second square with scenes from lands over yonder. According to Little Zander's reckoning, Canada was situated not far from the county borders. Africa, he believed, waited just beyond Canada's farthest edge. In Milton's picture, Canada was filled with grand houses and flowing rivers. Africa was home to tall mountains and cows grazing under a friendly sun. The people had great wings sprouting from their backs, and they smiled as they hovered above their fields and orchards.

The evening deepened, providing shadows that Milton could cling to as he headed to his family at Two Forks. He said his farewells and went night walking. Cato had retreated to our cabin, and I replaced him by leaning in the doorway. Little Zander paced excitedly between the two pictures, still visible in the moonlight. He chatted with himself as he moved, making notes and plans. A comfortable quiet settled among us.

Then Cupid reappeared. He swaggered out and stood in the middle of Milton's second drawing. He lowered the front of his pants and made water. Sighing with satisfaction, he splashed the African mountains and the dappled cows conjured from dust. The Buba Yalis, caught in the downpour, fell from the sky.

Zander shouted in protest. He rushed at Cupid, who swatted the boy away with a flick of his hand.

After Cupid finished relieving himself, he stood over Little Zander, who lay writhing on the ground.

"Boy, I have a notion to snap you like a twig."

"Not this night," I said, coming up behind him.

Cupid turned and grinned when he saw me. "Cannonball's pet. I do declare."

"That would be you. Likely you would eat from the palm of his hand."

"Are you challenging me?"

"Most certainly," I said. "But first, swear to me that you're sober."

"As a parson," Cupid said. He extended his hand, palm down, and raised it to the level of his shoulder. "See? Steady."

I nodded. "Good. You will have no excuse."

"You're gonna bleed for this," he said.

"Let's get at it, then."

Anyone who knew the two of us likely suspected that we were going to fight someday. Still, no one could say exactly when it would happen. The sun had never set on a day when Cupid wasn't cruel to men, women, and children alike. Although I was spared his bullying, it still made me sick to witness it. I felt, as had many men before me, that standing by silently while Cupid raged was as bad as doing his deeds myself. We had come close to blows often, only to have Greene step in with an order or Milton cool the air with a joke. Cupid's meanness to Zander that night was almost kind next to other things he had done. What made me challenge him then? What made him accept? It's a question I come back to nearly as often as I wonder about the runaway horse that crossed my path. Still, neither the horse nor anything else was on my mind when I readied myself to fight. I just wanted to make it back to the quarters in one piece.

As foreman, Cupid had Greene's permission to keep us in line with his fists, as long as we weren't too damaged to work the next day. Not often did any man have enough courage to face him down in the clearing. Those who did seldom returned on their feet. Cupid would swagger back, often in minutes, dragging his beaten foe behind him.

We left the quarters and went into the woods. In the space where Stolen brethren and sistren spent their Sundays singing, chanting, and praising the Ancestors, we faced each other with fists coiled. I abandoned my fighting stance and fished my knife from my pocket. I walked a few paces away and sank it into the ground.

"Yes," Cupid said. "Be of good courage. You will need every bit of it."

He was stronger, but I denied him the chance to seize his advantage. Instead I relied on my quickness to confound him, meeting each punch with a timelier effort of my own. My ribs shook with each blow he landed, but I stood my ground, determined to wear him down. Each second that we grappled felt like an hour. Finally a punch to his stomach provided me with an opening. When he doubled over, I dropped down and swept his legs from under him. He hit the ground, groaning. I folded his throat in the crook of my arm and squeezed until I thought my heart would burst from the effort. Cupid clawed at my wrist with two desperate hands, but I would not let go. His kicks grew fainter. His eyes rolled back in his head, and he went limp at last. I rose and stood over him, too weary to rejoice.

"You knew this moment would come," I said.

I turned away and bent from the waist. I hugged my knees and welcomed the rush of air into my heaving lungs. I hadn't just killed a man. I also had destroyed stolen property. Would they hang me? What punishment besides death could be added to a lifetime of hard labor? If they hanged me I'd never see Margaret again.

After some moments of hard breathing I heard a curious crackle behind me. I turned to see Cupid, alive as ever, hurrying toward me with my knife in his grip. He closed the distance quickly and reached me before I had time to react. I threw up a hand to protect myself. Meanwhile, Cato, having rushed into the clearing, had thrown his entire body. He soared above my head, holding on to a huge rock with his arms stretched out in front of him. The rock bounced against Cupid's head, and the big man dropped like stones tumbling from a chute. Cato went to his knees and slammed the rock down again and again. He staved in Cupid's skull but seemed not to notice, raising and smashing with a wildness I had not known was in his nature.

Finally I interrupted. "He's gone from there," I told him. "You're just beating bones now. We have to move."

Cato sat on the ground and stared at his hands.

Cato

~⦿~

Together we dragged Cupid's body deeper into the woods. I kept watch alone, huddled over the bones of my dead tormentor until William returned with two spades. We dug a grave even deeper than the stone pit in which we toiled, working quickly and silently. William asked me how many shirts I had. I told him two.

"After tonight you have only one," he said. "That one has to go with Cupid."

I looked down at my shirt and saw that blood covered most of it. I nodded, removed the shirt and threw it in. The night pressed heavily on my bare torso.

He paused after we rolled Cupid into the grave.

"What is it?"

"What you did, Cato. What you did for me. We're brothers now."

"I did it for me," I said. "And for Iris."

"Even so," William said. "Even so."

I was suddenly exhausted. I stuck my spade in the ground and leaned on it as if it were a crutch.

William did the same. "I had been mad at Cupid for a long time," he said. "Then I realized I was mad at myself for not helping you when you tussled with him before. I should have. I'm sorry."

"No," I said, shaking my head. "I needed to defend myself. To try."

We commenced filling in the grave. Between shovelfuls of dirt we considered how to account for Cupid's absence. We agreed that Greene would likely conclude that his foreman had run away in the night. He knew that Cupid had no friends among us and therefore might believe that he told no one of his plans.

"We can influence Greene's account by encouraging him to think it's his idea," William suggested. "Another tale of an ungrateful nigga who betrayed his master. We can shape this. It's all in the telling."

William

As we patted the earth smooth and covered it with brush, I remembered something Guinea Jack had told me. I repeated it to Cato.

"You know the worst thing a Thief can ever say to you?"

"You've been sold?"

"No. It's 'Let me tell you a story.' You hear those words, run."

II

Kingdoms

Greene dreamed of bottoms until, as usual, the screeching jarred him awake. His wife slept in her own room down the hall, but her voice was of such pitch and volume that mere walls could not contain it. He briefly considered investigating the cause of her distress—every day brought some new indignity—but chose instead to roll over and burrow underneath his pillow. If he had been in charge of designing the ideal woman, he had to admit, he would have included only some of his wife's best qualities. The lovely ivory of her skin, for example, at least those portions of her that thick layers of perfumed powders did not obscure. However, he would not have taken her voice into consideration. Because he believed that the fairer sex, like children, should be seen and not heard, he wasn't an admirer of women's voices in general. He did, however, acknowledge that some nigga wenches could sound almost angelic when they sang or hummed their unearthly hymns. If not for her age and her immensity, Silent Mary, his cook, could have come as close to the ideal woman as any. After all, she made delectable meals and never uttered a sound. Alas, she was one of a kind. The other wenches in his possession didn't screech, it was true. But they, too, could chatter and wail rapidly and loudly enough to ruin the calm of a quiet morning. Yes, their voices were as irritable as the females of his own species.

But their bottoms? They entered his imagination during idle moments. The way they undulated beneath their thin cotton shifts, as if moving to some irresistible rhythm. His planter friends agreed, with a touch of wonder and no little melancholy, especially after cards and pipes and whiskey, that there was something about a wench's hind parts that one couldn't turn away from. He had failed to turn away from Pandora one time too many, and his wife had banished her to the cookhouse. Now it was a new girl's task to stand over her bed all night, fanning her and whisking away flies. Already the dumb wretch had failed in her duties, nodding off and waking her mistress by falling to the floor with a loud *thump!* in the middle of the night. Greene's wife screeched (of course she did) and smashed her water pitcher over the girl's face, splitting her features unevenly. Her countenance was healing gradually, leaving a jagged seam as crooked and winding as the stream that coursed through the grounds of Placid Hall. The girl's general appearance was of no consequence to Greene, as long as her bottom achieved in full maturity the shapeliness it promised in youth.

Aside from her lopsided expression, the girl returned to her duties as passive and tame as before, seemingly untroubled by anything as worrisome as a thought. It puzzled Greene that even niggas built as sturdily as those in his possession could ultimately prove so weak. Perhaps no one would ever solve the debate about where exactly they fit on the Great Chain of Being. But blame for that failure could never be placed on men like himself, enlightened men of scientific bent who observed and experimented and carefully noted their conclusions for the benefit of posterity. Greene often marveled that Providence had blessed men like him with an entire continent of pliant, soulless beings, strong in body but empty in mind. Could the God who created him also have fashioned such abject failures? Greene, lately taken with polygenism, which argued that niggas were an entirely different species, considered it more likely that they also had an entirely different Creator. But didn't the Bible argue persuasively that there was only one God? Perhaps, as some contended, he made them explicitly to fetch and carry for their betters. Isn't that even what those befuddled abolitionists sometimes confessed, that God formed the niggas to serve and obey? How else to explain their superstitious natures, their frightfulness, their obsession with ghosts and babies born with cauls over their faces? In Greene's experience, every other nigga claimed to have the gift of second sight. He usually regarded his own lack of intuition as further evidence of his people's superiority, the infallibility of reason. But on that morning he would come to regret that, unlike niggas, he had no penchant for hunches. If he had woken with a feeling in his bones, he might have sensed somehow that Cupid was gone.

William

L ast night I dreamed I saw two angels wrestling a demon," Little Zander said. "A pair of Buba Yalis with beautiful black wings. When they beat their wings, the earth shook, the trees bent, and the wind howled. They were too much for that demon."

Zander spoke to me just before first light, outside our cabin. That's where I greeted him when I stumbled out and slowly straightened, doing my best to ignore the protests of my aching muscles. I could hear our people stirring inside cabins, stretching and muttering their sevens.

Zander stood in front of our cabin, staring toward the clearing. Shadows still hung thickly, preventing me from reading his expression. He nodded in response, idly scratching his scalp. "Reckon Cupid's sick," he said. "Don't you?"

"Why?" I asked.

"Well, it's just about first light and he's not here to put his hands on a body. To stand between us and the drinking gourd."

"Then why don't you help yourself to some water?"

"That's a notion," he said.

"Before you do, I want to hear more about your dream."

He glanced at me before returning his gaze toward the clearing. "As I said. Buba Yalis, two of them. With great black wings.

The demon was bigger than either of them, but they were too strong. Too much holy in them. At first it was one against one. They fought, rolling around in the dirt. The demon went down, but he got back up. That's when the second angel came. He put him down for good."

"Did you see their faces?"

He turned to me. I could make out his eyes, but he seemed to look beyond me, somewhere over my shoulder.

"William. You know how I know it was a dream?"

"How?"

"Good won too easy. Real life is harder than that. Even for angels."

Cato

We began to wonder before we even had words. As soon as we learned to toddle on our own two feet and feel the heaviness of the world, we began to ask ourselves why. Not why we were born but why we were born *there*. After we acquired the habits of speech, we joined the arguments everyone had, grown people and children alike. We bickered and squabbled about other places we'd heard of. Canada, Ohio, Africa, New Orleans. Some sounded much better than any places we'd known. Some sounded worse, although those were harder to conjure in our imaginations. But talk of other places, like any momentary pause that allowed us to reflect on our circumstances, eventually led us back to the bitter confines of Greene's terrible kingdom. Surely our purpose, our reason for being, had to be more than turning his timber into tables and chairs, putting up with his insistent groping, and grinding boulders into pebbles while he took notes.

The only time a man in my predicament didn't meditate on the how and the why of his captivity was when he had the good fortune to experience genuine love. Before she was sold off, Iris did that for me, helped me find a little space for myself in a world that had no use for me beyond the sweat of my brow, the strength of my back, and the skill in my weather-beaten hands.

Iris found other tasks for my hands. Sometimes we'd both be so sore, so afflicted with cuts and blisters that joining hands offered us more pain than comfort. Instead we'd find a spot behind a knuckle or close to the wrist that felt a little softer than the surrounding skin, and we'd stroke it just so. Iris liked to take my pointing finger and guide it over the contours of her face. She did it slowly and carefully, as if to reassure us both that a moment could exist outside the dispiriting routine of chop and tote and wipe and lift, that she and I were real and not just tick marks in a ledger book. When full of mischief, she would take that same rough finger and dip it into a cup of pot liquor. She would stir it around while staring into my eyes, the tip of her tongue poking wetly from her pursed lips. Then she would withdraw my finger, take a dramatic sip from her cup, and loudly sigh.

"So much better now," she would purr.

She made that soft, growling sound whenever I pleased her, which, to my great delight, was often. That a woman so wonderful could find something equally appealing in me never failed to astound me. I had known other women but only after tiresome campaigns for their attention. Unlike them, Iris boldly encouraged me from the start. Though Cupid had no knowledge of his role in our meeting, he was the one who brought us together.

He had earned a considerable amount of money for Greene by besting another Stolen in a fight. Many Thieves lusted for blood sport as fervidly as they pursued and brutalized Stolen women; they forced not only men but also hounds and roosters into mortal combat. Greene belonged in such company. Delighted with Cupid's triumph and his own swollen purse, he gave all of us a day's respite and convened with a feast, complete with fiddlers and Silent Mary's cooking. We left Placid Hall and joined Stolen from Pleasant Grove in a gathering at Two Forks, equidistant from Greene's other plantations. Many of us had never ventured from our respective places of captivity, and the chance to exchange stories with new acquaintances briefly warmed us. The next day, when we rose at first light under the unfamiliar burden of stuffed bellies and heads dizzy from too much dancing, when Cupid acted out his victory on our vulnerable hides, when the memory of fiddles buzzed at us like bees amid our onerous tasks, the evening's festivities would seem like just another form of torture, a spell summoned to remind us of our place in the world. But that would come later. The revelry lasted for hours. Under such circumstances, the illusion of freedom, however fleeting, can be as intoxicating as drink.

Pleasantly befuddled, I joined a group lined up for Silent Mary's cooking. I heard a woman call my name. Her eyes were as dark as coffee against her golden skin, unlike the luminous hazel often found in women of her complexion. She was slender and nearly as tall as me. Something about her bearing, the way she stood and gestured with one hip thrust slightly forward, suggested naughtiness, allure. I gave her my full attention.

"Is all that food just for you, Cato? Because you are surely blocking my way."

At first I thought she was making fun of me. She later told me she was simply helping me take note of her. I stepped aside to give her room. She remained where she was. "Pardon," I said. "How do you know my name?"

"I know plenty," she replied, smiling. Her grin was surprisingly wide, almost out of place on her delicate, oval face. She had a gap between her two front teeth.

"Are you from Placid Hall, Cato?"

I nodded, thinking that she had to know I was from there, especially if she knew all that she claimed. "Yes," I said. "Like everyone else here, I belong to Cannonball Greene."

She purred at me for the first time and made a clucking noise with her tongue. "Not anymore," she said. "From this day on, you belong to me."

Greene allowed us to keep company whenever it didn't inconvenience him. With his permission, I endeavored to make Iris a stool from leftover wood. She had developed a habit of sitting on the humble stoop in front of her cabin at Two Forks and resting on cool evenings. Although I revered the ground she sat upon, I deemed it unworthy of her touch. Nothing cheered me more than seeing her perched on that stool as I approached. At the time I knew nothing of queens, of royal figures perched regally on thrones. But I knew that my Iris possessed nobility that far surpassed her lowly surroundings. I would sit at her feet grateful for the simple gift of her attention—until we entered her cabin.

To speak much of our private moments would deny Iris the dignity that her memory deserves. May it suffice to say that she created in me a lightness of heart of which I had not thought myself capable. Our interludes provided me with a glimpse of marvels I'd yet to know, treasures I could claim for my own in another place, somewhere yonder.

After she was taken from me, scenes from that magical place returned when I neither wanted nor expected them. I would be sanding lumber into planks or washing myself at the trough and suddenly find myself peering into another world where the air belonged to every man, where each step I took was in the fulfillment of my own desire. But in those dreamlike intervals I walked alone, as certain of Iris's absence as I was of my own freedom. What good could become of me without her by my side?

I shook off those intrusions like a hound ridding itself of fleas, replacing them with memories in which Iris was fully present. Once, when we were reclining comfortably in each other's arms, I asked her to name her favorite color.

"Whatever color you are," she said.

"Iris, tell me. Your favorite color. Describe it to me."

"I'd say you're about the same as polished walnut. I saw you rubbing that stool you'd made me. You insisted on making it gleam before I could sit down on it. I remember you with that cloth, rubbing. I couldn't tell where your hand ended and the wood began. Polished walnut."

"Iris. Just tell me."

She rolled over and faced me.

"Cato, *you're* my favorite, and that's as far as I go with it. Declaring my fondness for things means I got to feel the hurt when they're taken away. Nothing good lasts."

"I'm going to last," I told her. "I swear it on my seven words."

"Good," she said, grinning again. "The only thing I've let my heart linger on is you."

That wasn't completely true. She kept mementos of the people she'd lost. A patch of straw from an old hat. A yank of hair from a baby who had been sold. She kept those things in a pouch hanging from a cowhide string around her waist, as was the habit of many Stolen women. She never talked much about her departed loves, but I knew they lived in her heart too. After we lay together for the first time, she put stray locks from my beard into her pouch. I found myself grateful that she had made room for me.

Nestled against her, I learned more about the two children she'd borne and lost. About the straw hat her mother took off her head and handed to her before new Thieves yanked her away. How Iris wore it until the sun burned through its tattered fringe. Her stammers and pauses showed me how hard it was for her to talk about the people she loved and who had loved her. They remained mostly a part of her private self.

The night we put Cupid in the ground, Iris slept beside me once more. We remained together until morning, something we had never been able to do. Before she left my cabin, she removed her pouch from her waist and tossed it to me. I caught it and pressed it to my lips. When I woke my hands were empty, and of course Iris was gone. I was staring into my palms, still struggling to make sense of the dream, when Greene stormed into the quarters.

William

My cabinmates and I slept longer than usual and woke to the sound of screaming. We were used to hearing Screech Owl wailing in the distance, but the shriek was not hers. Cato was already awake, gazing into his open hands as if lost in a dream. Milton sat up.

"Nila," he said.

Although we were more than familiar with Nila's moans, we had never gotten used to them. Cupid managed to find new ways to hurt her, and it always wounded us to hear the result.

"Damn that Cupid," Milton continued. "Damn him."

Unlike Milton, I knew that Cupid was not the cause of her torment. No, the source of her torment was in fact dead in the ground. For a terrifying second I feared he had climbed out of his grave and returned, vengeance on his mind.

I stepped outside, my cabinmates at my heels. We found Greene dragging Nila the length of the quarters by her hair, his fist clutching her locks like the handle of a carpetbag. He stopped in front of the water trough and pulled her to her knees. Her dress, barely a rag to begin with, was torn to strips that barely covered her. Dirt ran in streaks from her forehead to her bare feet. One side of her mouth was swollen where he must have slapped her.

We trotted to a halt before Greene.

"Where is he, Nila?"

"I don't know. He been gone all night. I swear I ain't seen him."

"If you're lying to me, bitch, I'll twist your head clean off."

"No, suh, I swear."

He yanked Nila upward, only to smack her to the ground in a single motion.

"William," he said, turning to me, "I want men looking for him at every farm. I've already sent for Tanner and Kirk. They should be here presently. You and the pit gang will help them search the woods. That nigga better turn up. He can be blind, crippled, or crazy but he needs to show his black hide soon. It has never been hard to make that nigga happy. A swig of scotch and a wench. That's all he ever needed. I have given him more than he could dream of. All he had to do was get the best of another buck once in a while. Keep the rest of you niggas in order. And he has the gumption to run on me?"

Dr. LeMaire arrived in a huff, interrupting Greene's tirade, panting and looking perturbed. The doctor, whom I had met long ago in the log pen with Norbrook, visited from time to time to care for Screech Owl.

We waited until Greene turned his full attention to LeMaire before moving. Cato went to Nila. He helped her to a sitting position and rubbed her back. I sent Little Zander running to the cookhouse for Pandora.

"He was supposed to meet me early," Greene said to LeMaire. "I told him to come round at first light after rousing the others. He and I had an engagement in Warren County, a tussle with a buck. Cupid would have taken him, I'm sure. Now he's disappeared and I've lost my deposit. No need to even think about the prize money. It's out of my hands."

Less than an hour later, we surveyed the woods just beyond Greene's borders. There were four of us, two on each side of the Thieves astride their mounts. Little Zander took a deep breath.

"It's different," he said. "Feels different inside me, this air."

"It's not free air," I told him.

He smiled and shook his head. "I know that. But I'm a step closer to it all the same. Too bad Milton isn't here to breathe it in. He could make a picture for us later."

I understood what Zander meant. There was a chance we'd never get this far out again. We could have stored each image in our memories, the endless trees, the sun burning through the foliage in fierce streams of orange and red, the fussy babble of birds, and the scurrying of animals we could hear but not see. We could have called the scenes up again later, argued about the details, whether a gentle breeze was blowing, whether the lumpy tree that Tanner and Kirk called the Weeping Woman actually looked like a woman, or if it was really bear scat that Cato had slipped in. But Milton seeing it with us would have been as good as preserving it all in stone. On nights when our backs were too sore to let us sleep or the heat simply too insistent for rest, he could have taken up a stick and begun to stir in the dirt and sure enough it would have all come back. But he had stepped on a fallen branch the night before, during his return from seeing Sarah and the baby. A splinter, Milton had called it, but the wedge of wood buried in his heel was surprisingly thick and long. Silent Mary had dug it out, and there had been considerable blood. Greene, displeased, finally agreed that Milton was better off laid up than hunting a runaway. Besides myself, that left Cato, Double Sam, and Little Zander. Although Sam was a reliable enough worker, his constant muttering made anything beyond idle chatter a chore. He was born a twin, but his brother had lived only a few hours. Sam talked to him all the time nonetheless, explaining to anyone who asked that he was simply continuing a discussion the siblings had begun in the womb.

He had slim, nimble fingers like a fiddler, with unblemished knuckles and nails free of the cracks and stains typically found among us. In the years since, I've often imagined him in a crowded concert hall, adjusting his waistcoat before touching his bow to the strings. In reality, he was a man far more comfortable with animals than with people. He had mastered the tools of his trade, the halter, the rein, the right words to chant in a yearling's ears. We'd all witnessed the miracle of cows giving more milk and chickens laying more eggs simply because he was standing nearby. His presence calmed the horses as we continued our search for traces of Cupid.

While we fended off the slapping branches and fought our way through the clouds of black flies swarming about our necks, I wished that Double Sam had the same easeful effect on Cato. We had passed Cupid's hidden grave without incident. Deeper into the woods, though, Cato spent some moments as jittery as a colt. At other moments he slowed down and stared at his hands as if they were a stranger's.

I felt the urge to shake him roughly, but I feared my actions would be as likely to attract the interest of Tanner and Kirk as Cato's strange behavior would. Worried that he would give us away, I stayed between him and the two Thieves as often as I could. Little Zander's constant darting about made it no easy task.

At the next opportunity, I touched Cato on the shoulder and asked him what he was feeling.

"Despair," he said.

I fixed my eyes on his. "Of all the things we can ill afford, that would be uppermost."

He wiped his brow and breathed deeply, as if considering what I'd said.

"We come from Strong," I reminded him.

He nodded. "Strong," he repeated. "Strong."

"Good. And stop looking at your hands."

We hadn't gone much farther when Tanner's horse appeared to pull up lame. He dismounted and beckoned Double Sam. The two of them spoke briefly before Tanner handed over the reins. Double Sam guided the gimpy animal to a shade tree a few yards ahead of us.

"What's the trouble?" Kirk asked.

"Don't know," Tanner replied. "Double Sam is seeing to him."

"That ornery beast of yourn. He lets you down too much. I'd have put him to pasture by now."

Tanner pulled his hat low over his brow. "No need. He's got plenty of miles left in him."

At a sign from Tanner, Cato and I dropped our sacks and sat down in the grass. Zander stayed on his feet, pacing. Tanner strolled into a copse to make water.

From what I'd gathered from the Thieves' conversation, Kirk had planned to spend the day sleeping off a night of drunken carousing. Instead he was glaring red-eyed under a blistering sun, chasing a runaway. He slid off his mount, grunting.

"Got me a notion," he said turning to me. Overwhelmed by his stench, I struggled to keep my face expressionless.

"I'm thinking I could leave these two jumpy niggas in the woods and report them as runaways. I could say they skittered off while you other two were seeing to Tanner's horse."

He pointed to Cato, then to Little Zander, an action that required him to raise his arm. I choked down the bile rising in my throat.

"Then I'd get me three rewards, one for the each of ya and 'nuther for Cupid. That big nigga couldn't have got fur. Likely even drowned in a crick or else got et by a bear. In that case I'd just bring back a piece of his hide."

I was preparing to shrug helplessly at Kirk when the sound of Double Sam's bickering distracted him.

Sam was arguing with his brother. "I know when a horse is about to be done," he said. "Is that right? How many horses have you handled? You don't know a horse from a cow, even when you're looking over my shoulder. Give me some room. I can't work with you breathing on my neck."

Kirk scratched himself and spat. "Good Lord," he said. "Damned if Cannonball Greene doesn't have the craziest collection of niggas in the entire county. I have a notion how to fix this one."

He hurried off toward Double Sam, but Tanner emerged from the copse and met him halfway.

Cato and I rose to our feet. Little Zander joined us as we watched the Thieves talk.

"Think we're far from Africa?" Zander asked me.

"I don't spend much time thinking about Africa. Every time I pause to think I end up with stripes on my back."

"I think about it a lot," Zander said. "In the morning, after I say my seven, I say the word over and over. *Africa. Africa.* Just like that. It's a notion I got from Milton. You know what else he told me, William? He said you don't believe in anything."

I watched Kirk throw up his hands, turn away from Tanner, and move in our direction. "I'll tell you what I believe," I said. "I believe we have five minutes or less before that foul-smelling Thief starts thinking again about how small his life is and how he can forget about his smallness for a while by crushing the joy out of the only thing smaller. That's us."

I was exhausted. Whatever beauty the day possessed when we started out had faded. The mere thought of the trek back under a stubborn sun just made me more tired. Weariness marked us in our sagging postures, the gradual slowing of our motions. I could see it in the horses. I could see it in Kirk's shortened stride as he sauntered back to us.

Zander wasn't tired. He bounded around in little leaps that grew larger until finally he began to flip and tumble, cartwheeling across the grass. When Kirk got close enough, he aimed his rifle at the boy and pretended to shoot him.

"Bang!" he said, cackling. "You a fast one, ain't cha? Jumpin' around like a jackrabbit. But you cain't outrun this here gun. Want to try? How 'bout we have ourselfs a race?"

Little Zander stopped and balanced on one leg, his heel resting on his opposite knee. He looked uncertainly at Kirk.

"Mebbe we bes' be gittin' on," I said. "Afore Cupid gets too far to track."

Kirk looked at me, stroking the barrel of his gun. "I makes my livin' huntin' niggas, nigga. You fixin' t' tell me how to do my job?"

"Nawsuh, boss," I replied. "Nawsuh."

"Good. Right smart of you." He spat.

From the corner of my eye I saw Cato looking at his hands. He looked up at Kirk, then back to his hands, as if he had a notion to wrap them around the Thief's throat. I caught his eye and shook my head.

Tanner and Double Sam arrived with Tanner's mount. Sam held the reins in one hand and stroked the horse's flank with the other.

"What's wrong with him?" Kirk demanded. "He broke down?"

"Nawsuh," Double Sam replied. "He just discouraged. He done for the day, boss."

"He's right," Tanner said. "Best we head back."

"Damn it all," Kirk said. "And we ain't seen hide nor hair."

"The trail is cold because there is no trail," Tanner told him. "If he ran he didn't run this way."

"Maybe he flew," Little Zander whispered to me as we turned and prepared to head back to Placid Hall.

"Hush, Zander."

He laughed softly. "I'm not scared of that Kirk. *Angel* is watching."

"What?"

Zander pointed overhead. "In the trees."

I paused and studied the branches overhead. All I saw was the steady sunlight, leaves bending and twisting, and one stubborn squirrel, staring down at the giants tramping rudely beneath his perch.

Pandora

I have never gotten used to flies. Their buzzing is an abomination, their appearance hideous, and their touch repugnant. They gathered in clumps at Placid Hall, so often that it was rare indeed to see a solitary fly perched on a porch rail, rubbing its forelegs or devouring a crumb. I found it remarkable that other Stolen could get so lost in their labors that they appeared not to notice them. The flies landed on the backs of necks, alighted on knuckles, even crawled across eyelids—and still my people worked, either oblivious or amazingly disciplined. Not me. I hated flies then and detest them still.

Their ugliness, their outright unruliness, made them seem out of place in the great outdoors where so much of nature is beautiful. Even dangerous things can be a delight to behold, like snakes with their jeweled skins, or poisonous plants with lovely leaves. When standing under Screech Owl's window and straining beneath her slop jar, I still found plenty to marvel at. As my back ached and my outstretched arms began to tremble, I could find comfort in a redbird splashing in a puddle or perhaps a cottontail springing behind a bush.

On the worst days, nothing in nature could offer me respite. The flies circled above my head expectantly, as if waiting for my knees to buckle and listening for the command to turn the jar upon myself. Then they would descend, sticking to me, blinding me, crawling into my ears and nostrils, seeking my lips and teeth as I raced for the stream, stinking of Screech Owl's rotten insides. They gave chase until I was fully immersed, an angry throng swirling above the surface of the stream while I washed away every remnant of filth from my skin.

If the natural splendor of my surroundings failed to bring relief, I fancied myself elsewhere. For example, while boiling the clothes, other Stolen sweated. Not me. I was far away, in a great gilded carriage pulled by six white horses, surveying my vast holdings while a servant knelt in front of me and polished the buckles on my shoes. And yet somehow I still tended the laundry, stirring the pot, mixing the lye.

I learned about faraway kingdoms during my first eight harvests, when I was a playmate for a young Thief named Lillian. Missy, as I was encouraged to call her, was the beloved daughter of a wealthy landowner who spared no expense to make her happy. It was Missy's pleasure to have me dressed in the finest linens, and I was never far from her at any point in the day. Our hours were filled with merriment, song, and sweets that seemed to stream from the cookhouse in an endless supply. There were joyless moments when Missy caused some impertinence—a broken goblet or a muddied frock—and I was punished in her stead. Whippings and the denial of supper were a small price to pay for the luxury that seemed my birthright. We played with dolls, ordered the servants around, and enjoyed daily tea parties. Standing hand in hand in front of the great looking glass in her room, we often marveled at how much we resembled the other.

"We could be sisters, dear Pandora," Missy would say. "Only you look as if you'd had a bit more sun."

Because I had no memory of any other place, I often felt that Missy's world belonged to me as much as to her. The Thieves of the house had long discouraged me from asking questions about my origins. Missy's governess, Mrs. Knox, a formal woman with a stiff posture and a foreign accent, suggested that I had arrived at their back door in the manner of a foundling from a fairy tale, whisked from some mysterious land in a cloud of stars and gossamer ribbons. Glory, the cook, was the closest to a mother I had. She, too, advised me to refrain from thinking about the past and focus instead on my most fortunate present. I had not yet understood the distinctions between Stolen and Thieves (perhaps I didn't want to). The servants in the main house mostly shared my complexion. I'd seldom had contact with the field hands. They'd had, to borrow Missy's words, more than a bit of sun.

On one occasion, Glory sent me near the quarters to fetch some herbs from a friend of hers who worked in the fields. I found the woman waiting with the requested items wrapped in a knot of cloth. She seemed quite fretful, as if she feared being caught and chastised for some violation. I remember less of her features than I do her nervousness, which was of such intensity that it was contagious. Despite the brevity of our exchange, I found myself becoming anxious as well.

Our hands touched, and she grabbed mine with a sudden ferocity. I cried out and pulled mine away.

"Please," she said. "Don't be afraid. Please. I just want to look at you. Please."

Two more field hands appeared and forcefully escorted her down the row leading to the cabins. Every few steps she turned and gazed at me longingly.

I was puzzled, perhaps even a little frightened. In subsequent years I have concluded that the woman may have been my mother. At the time I knew enough to keep the specifics of the unsettling encounter to myself.

"Wherever have you been," Missy demanded, when I returned to her company in the nursery. "Mrs. Knox is about to read a story."

I folded my skirts and joined Missy at Mrs. Knox's feet. I was never allowed to look at the words on a page for long, and of course as I grew my opportunities to actually hold a book in my hands ceased altogether. I was not moved to protest, preferring instead to imagine what the story described. My own fanciful scenes, featuring princesses who looked like me, filled in the pauses in Mrs. Knox's narration. They did the same on many an evening, when the governess again read to Missy before settling her down for sleep. Afterward I curled up on the floor at the foot of Missy's bed, warm and snug under a beautiful embroidered blanket. Some nights she would invite me to climb into her bed with her, giggling and confiding as little girls do, until at last slumber claimed us.

It all ended when Missy took sick and died in the course of a week. A plague swept through the county, claiming young and old alike. A remedy the Stolen had concocted from the roots of particular plants had enabled most of them to escape the sickness. But their homemade medicine was unknown in the big house, where Missy became feverish and weak.

Mrs. Knox brought me to her sickbed when there was little time left. I could do little but cry and tell Missy that I loved her.

She had never seemed so small before. Dark circles ringed her eyes, and the thin slash of her mouth had swollen to a bruised pucker. Her voice, always so shrill and girlish, had aged dramatically and was now more like a whisper or a creak. She took hold of my hand with surprising strength.

"Why do I have the sickness, Pandora?" she asked. "Why me and not you?"

When her life ended, mine went from heavenly to hellish in the course of a single afternoon. Missy had no sooner breathed her last when I was seized and roughly taken by a nephew who had often lurked about the place. I had thought him quite kind, as he was fond of riding me on his shoulders and plying me with sweets. The encounter left me marked in more ways than I can count, seemingly establishing for me a lifetime of torture as a plaything of Thieves.

The lady of the house, nearly mad from grief and simmering jealousies, was only too eager to get rid of me. She sold me to the first trader passing through. At first I thought my sale to him resulted purely from chance. Later I convinced myself that she had knowledge of his commerce in illicit pleasures, that she knew exactly what I would have to suffer and endure. While surviving ordeals of sufficient horror to provoke a grown man to curl up and die, I sometimes wondered what she'd done with the coins she'd received for selling me away. What had she purchased with her profit? A shiny goblet? A new frock?

To keep myself from falling completely into madness, I learned to live in two worlds. Flat on my back or writhing in chains, I cavorted with elves and pixies, princesses and fairy godmothers. I marveled at servant girls transformed into dazzling beauties in gleaming castles. I wondered at enchanted woodland creatures as they provided timely assistance to damsels in distress. I thrilled at the sight of pumpkins turning into chariots and straw magically becoming heaps of glittering gold. My imaginary haven sometimes became so real that the intrusion of my actual circumstances left me dumbstruck. As a result, I was often a disappointment, unable to fulfill the yearnings of the Thieves who visited our traveling enterprise with fat purses and perverse expectations. I became cheap currency. It has often been said that women with my pallor were considered more desirable than my sun-kissed sisters but nothing in our experience confirmed this. After all, we were all similarly constructed beneath our clothes. But neither our nakedness nor our comeliness was the deciding factor. What moved Thieves most was the cold fact of our vulnerability: our men couldn't protect us. Nor could we protect ourselves.

I seldom thought of dashing knights or charming princes during my travails. Of all the characters from Missy's ever-after stories, I found them least likely to have counterparts in real life. By the time I had arrived at Placid Hall I had seen the worst of men, the foulest of their appetites and capabilities. That they could also have good qualities often seemed too rich to believe, even for an imagination as ravenous as mine.

In the big house with the Greenes, it was easier to sustain my fantasies. I had to work harder to build my dream worlds after Screech Owl sent me into exile. Gone was the cool interior of my castle chambers, made so by my half-dozen attendants waving huge, feathery fans, replaced by the smoke and heat of Silent Mary's cookhouse. Gone was the immense bath where I reclined for hours eating sweets, replaced by the steam of the laundry kettles. I did my best to work and live unnoticed, my secret life tucked away.

It was part of our daily labors to anticipate the moods of the Thieves who oppressed us. Often we had but seconds to determine whether they were lonely or sad enough to engage a Stolen in civil conversation, whether we should lend an ear or be as stiff and insensitive as furniture. Whether to step left or right to avoid collision, whether to move past them quickly or remain still so their hands could roam. I wondered if all Stolen had an entirely different existence hidden behind those extravagant courtesies, one that they dared not share with anyone. I was most curious about Cato, the man with the thoughtful hands. What was he thinking about? What had he lost?

I had wondered the same about Nila as I tended her wounds. She said little, rocking and humming to herself between sips of a broth Silent Mary had made for her. Nila's man had run away and left her behind, a man who hadn't seemed to care much for her in the first place. I thought maybe she was relieved, but it was too soon to venture the notion. I knew from experience that Stolen sometimes fled without telling the people closest to them. The less they knew, the less they could tell. Thieves never saw it that way. In their view, Stolen always knew more than they let on. They could seldom prove it, but they were willing to exhaust themselves and us by beating out of us information that didn't exist. Cannonball Greene was no exception.

In the hours that passed since he sent out search parties, his anger had somehow grown. He came back to the quarters, smelling of drink and throwing questions at Nila all over again. But she had withdrawn into herself and said even less than before. Enraged, Greene began to berate her and cuff her about the ears. He stopped suddenly, realizing that he had left home without his brandy. He sent me to retrieve his snifter. I nearly spilled the brandy when Screech Owl kicked me as I left the servants' entrance, sending me staggering straight into a cloud of flies. I was bringing the drink to Greene on a silver tray when I heard Nila's pitiable groans.

She had fallen to the ground at Greene's feet and was mumbling pleas for mercy. He shoved her away roughly with his boot. I knew to stand within arm's reach and wait silently while he spat curses at her shivering form. As I stood and balanced the tray, I spotted a rescue party approaching from the distance, including a gilded carriage with a footman, flanked by a pair of knights. A fairy godmother, I guessed, or a wealthy dowager finally about to locate her long-lost heir.

Hold on, I wanted to tell Nila. *Rescue is coming, perhaps for both of us.*

My hopes faded as the arriving party got closer. The carriage became two horses, one bearing a rider and the other being led by a Thief on foot. Four Stolen men accompanied them. Cato, William, Zander, and Double Sam. Even at that distance I could make out their distinctive gaits. I didn't know the names of the Thieves but guessed they were the paddy rollers Tanner and Kirk. I'd heard much about those men, none of it encouraging. To make matters worse, Cupid wasn't with them.

Greene left us and met the searchers at the entrance to Placid

Hall, a good three hundred paces away. After conferring with them he returned at a rapid clip, the men not far behind. He tried to pull Nila up from the ground, but she refused to rise.

"Very well," Greene said. "I'll drag you."

He grabbed her by the hair, just as he had that morning. At once I discovered his intent. He meant to take her to the whipping post.

Cato stepped forward while Nila screamed and struggled in Greene's grasp.

"Please, boss," he said. "I don't think she can take another beatin'."

"I'll thank you to forgo thinking," Greene said.

William advanced cautiously, hands raised. "Boss," he said. "She don't know. If she did, she'd tell you."

Greene chuckled. I could tell by William's face that he could smell the spirits on him.

"Best you be meek now," Greene warned. "You're not as costly as you suppose."

The taller of the paddy rollers cleared his throat and spat. "Respectfully, Mr. Greene," he said, "why we still talkin'? We all know what that wench is up to. She's tarryin' so as to help that nigga. He likely halfway ta Canada or somewhere. Stupid buck will be turned into a fur collar on account of us jawin' with this wench instead of puttin' stripes on her."

He smelled as strongly as Greene, but not of liquor.

"All right, Kirk," Greene said. He turned to the other paddy roller. "What about you, Tanner? I've been beating her all day, and she's said nothing."

Tanner studied Nila a long moment. "It's your property," he said. "You should have final say."

"That settles it," Greene said. "Zander, fetch the whip."

"I'll shuck her for you," Kirk said, scratching himself. "Skin her too."

"Shucking and tying will suffice," Greene said. He grabbed the drink from the tray and gulped it down. "As for the whipping, I'll do it myself."

He released his grip on Nila's hair. With the other hand he replaced the glass on the tray. I turned my body toward the gates of Placid Hall, away from the whipping post. They usually made us watch whenever a Stolen got punished, but Greene hadn't yet ordered us to do anything. I was determined not to see Nila beaten unless he made me. I stared into the distance, as far as I could see, where Greene's borders met the sky and the heat waves fluttered above the ground like gossamer ribbons.

Somewhere in Nature there are castles, I thought. *Somewhere there is magic and gold.*

Cato

I heard Greene say he'd do the whipping. I watched him grab the drink and swallow it. While he drank, I imagined my hands moving of their own accord. I saw them reaching for Greene's throat and the Thieves raising their guns to shoot us down. I felt my thumbs go in, the satisfying crunch and snap, before the weapons roared. To still my hands, to save us all, I spoke up.

"It's not her," I said. "It's me. Cupid tol' me he was gon' run. Tol' me not to tell."

I could feel Tanner and Kirk gazing hotly at my back, the astonished silence of the other Stolen. Greene tarried a moment before turning to glare at me.

"Again," he ordered. "Tell me again what you just said. Tell me again what possessed you to withhold a confidence from your master."

"I reckon I don't know," I told him. "I was so afeared of Cupid."

Greene grinned. It was ugly to see. "Oh, you don't know fear." He nodded at Kirk over my shoulder. I turned in time to see the rifle stock rushing toward my face.

After they pickled Isaac for running to his beloved, he refused to eat or drink. His hair fell out, then his teeth. He held on to a peach pit that in his madness he began to call Oney. All of us wondered where he got it because peaches were reserved exclusively for the residents of the big house. In frustration, our Thief placed him in irons in front of his cabin for all the Stolen to bear witness to his long, excruciating death. But someone took mercy on him and smothered him in the night.

A chain around my neck connected me to the post, inches from where I had told Greene that I was the one who had protected Cupid's secret. My wrists and ankles were similarly bound, though my pain alone was sufficient to keep me confined. I didn't know how long I had been there, but the occasional hoot of an owl and hounds baying in the distance told me that night had fallen hours before. When I heard Isaac mumbling in my ear as I lay next to the whipping post, I was too exhausted to be afraid. I deduced— perhaps wished—that Isaac had come from somewhere yonder to put me out of my misery, just as a kind soul had done for him.

"Best be still," he advised. "Moving won't help you any. Trust me, I know."

Too sore even to open my eyes or turn toward the sound of his voice, I had no choice but to heed his suggestion. My efforts to speak were equally fruitless. With my tongue swollen and my mouth filled with blood, all I could manage was a grunt. Every inch of my flesh felt aflame, as if Greene had turned me on a spit above an open fire. What had he done to me?

Isaac responded as if he could hear my thoughts.

"Pickled you, of course," he explained. "Slashed you from top to bottom, and then seized you by the feet and dunked you head-long in a barrel of brine. Reckon you can hardly remember. That's best."

I had never been much for crying. To my view it served lit-tle purpose, likely to inspire renewed cruelty in men like Cupid. And Thieves like Greene, accustomed to wrenching suckling babes from their mothers' breasts, regarded our tears as resulting from some primitive animal instinct and not from genuine emotion. In their eyes, all our wounds were temporary inconveniences from which we would soon recover. However, as waves of agony overtook me, I was moved to part my lips and wail as helplessly as an orphan in a storm. But my voice betrayed me, as it often did. Instead of hurling protests to the night sky, I was left to convulse with silent sobbing. Many times I thought myself in the throes of death, only to arrive at a brief respite before beginning to die again.

Isaac waited patiently until my twitching eased and I finally opened my eyes. He remained behind me, out of sight. I imagine he was squatting on his haunches like a man watching over a pile of sticks, coaxing smoke from ash and embers.

"You need to rest," he said. "Sleep will help. Staying awake just makes you consider how much better dying would be. But you would be wrong. Don't make the mistake I made."

I felt Isaac slide his hand under my head, his rough palm scraping my battered skull. Once more I was moved to scream, but I was still out of air, out of sound. I found just enough strength to turn away when he held a gourd to my lips. He tried again—and again I refused.

"Come now, Cato," he chided. "You need this water." He sighed and lowered my head back to the ground.

For a moment I no longer sensed his presence. Then he returned with a damp rag and gently swiped my brow.

"You are being rude, friend," he said. "Downright uncivil. Remember the rules."

I squeezed my eyes shut, although it hurt to do so. I wanted to tell him that he knew nothing of the rules of civility.

He chuckled. "Don't be so certain. Listen to this: 'Drink not, nor talk with your mouth full, neither gaze about while you are drinking.'"

I wanted to cover my ears, but the chains prevented me. Isaac continued, ignoring my efforts.

" 'Drink not too leisurely, nor yet too hastily,' " he whispered, as if reciting from a book. " 'Before and after drinking, wipe your lips; breathe not them or ever with too great a noise, for it is uncivil.' "

I gasped and grunted as robustly as I could in a feeble attempt to overwhelm his voice. He spoke louder, his volume rising in accord with an immense spasm of pain. My consciousness was ebbing.

"Be not resigned to a life of suffering," Isaac suggested. "Keep your eyes on the days ahead."

There was no such rule, I wanted to tell him.

"And this one to observe above all others. Do not quit."

Those were the last words I heard before oblivion descended.

Margaret

Greene sent Nila back to Two Forks after Cato's confession. Although she had been spared a whipping, her face and body showed signs of punishment. In the cabin she would share with Sarah and me, we stayed awake with her into the night, thinking our attention would comfort her.

We sat in near darkness, our only light a few thin moonbeams seeping through the cracks in our walls. We were tempted to set fire to a pine knot and stick it in a cleft, but Holtzclaw, the driver man, sometimes saw a flickering flame as an invitation.

I worried for William and Cato. Nila seemed to think something had happened between them. They had exchanged a look, she said, when Greene sent them on their luckless search for Cupid. She told us about Cato stepping forward to take the blame. A paddy roller had smashed his gun against Cato's head before they dragged him off to torture him.

We encouraged her to get finished with her crying before the next day began. Holtzclaw, hired to oversee Greene's operation with an unrelenting meanness, was likely to be impatient with her, despite her bruises. She shook and sobbed, but her eyes remained dry. Our offers to hold her were soundly refused. Sarah and I quickly understood that she preferred to hug herself. I retreated to my pallet while Sarah looked after her daughter, sleeping in a crude cradle in the corner farthest from the door. Perched on a stool at our table, Nila rested her head on the table's surface, her arms folded underneath her. Because I hadn't known much about her before Cupid had claimed her, I couldn't help wondering what kind of woman she'd been. Watching her, I guessed that her former self had been scoured away, lost forever. I wondered how long she could hold up in the fields.

"Holtzclaw will likely set you to picking first thing," I told her. "You'll want to pace yourself."

Nila didn't move. "I've been in the fields before," she said.

"We're just saying that maybe you're not used to all the work he's been putting on us," Sarah said.

She sat up directly. "You think what I've been doing isn't work? How about you trade places with me, then? See if you last a day. See if you last an hour."

No one spoke for several long minutes. Crickets chirped outside, their song buoyed by an occasional breeze. Finally Sarah broke the silence.

"He didn't tell you?"

"Tell me what?"

"That he was going to run."

"You don't have to worry about us saying anything," I said. "You know us better than that."

"I don't know what I know. I'm grateful to you for tending to me, I am. But I got nothing to share besides the knowledge that I didn't mean a thing to Cupid. I might as well have been a hole in the ground."

"It's not my place," Sarah said, "but I will ask. Was Cupid never kind? He never talked softly to you?"

Nila sucked her teeth. "You're right, it's not your place. He got blood in his eye when he was a boy. Ruined him for kindness."

"That was just talk," I said. "Nobody believes—"

"Hmph. Spend your nights under a man like him, spend your days keeping out of his way. Then tell me what you believe."

We talked, sometimes arguing and sometimes consoling, until weariness of mind and body got the best of us. Before falling asleep I asked our Ancestors to keep watch over Nila in the fields. She would have to step carefully with Holtzclaw, just as she had done with Cupid. The two men had much in common, despite one being a Thief and the other Stolen. On the worst days, Holtzclaw would stare so hard you thought your dress might catch fire. He would stare until finally you had to meet his gaze, and he would shift his head just a little, in the direction of the barn. You knew that meant to drop your sack and go with him. I had been under Greene's protection since he paired me with William. Still, I slept with a shard near my pallet just in case.

Cato

I awoke to flies buzzing and the sun's heat finding every crack in my body. My bones felt as if they had tangled and knotted while I curled against the post in fitful sleep. I had no strength to move; it hurt just to consider it. Isaac was right: being still was best.

"Cato. Cato. Are you still with us?"

"He is. If he wasn't, an angel would have come and taken him away."

I recognized the voices of William and Little Zander. I felt Zander's hand against my neck.

"He's still here," he said. "Just like I told you."

"Cato," William said. "Greene's giving you three days. You can live or die. We want—I want—you to live."

I felt a gourd being pressed to my lips. I kept my mouth shut tight.

"Come on," Zander urged. "Take some water."

I tried to shake my head, but I'm not sure if I moved at all.

Their voices faded. I heard murmurs, whispered arguments. Then they slowly drew near, each step resounding in my head like a fist pounding a drum.

Before I could adjust to those violent vibrations, I was drenched. Torrents of water bombarded me, shocking me from

96

my scalp to my toes. Water found the cracks in my body as surely as the sun's rays had, flooding my nose and ears while battering my eyelids. The deluge seemed to continue for hours, but in reality it only lasted until William and Little Zander finished emptying their upturned pails.

I coughed and snorted and rolled away as far as my chains allowed me, prompting a new succession of searing cramps and stings.

"We're not going to let you die," William yelled. I heard him hurl a pail to the ground and stomp away.

Zander knelt down and spoke softly in my ear. "The Buba Yalis are busy enough," he said. "Don't give them any bother."

I don't know how long I lay there, inert and unmindful of the world's mad whirling. When I could finally open my eyes without wishing for death, I found myself staring at the stars. Behind them the sky was awash in blackness, cool comfort after the sweltering sunlight that had tormented me all day. I heard movement and turned to see Pandora emerge out of the dark. She squatted and stared, her face unsmiling.

"Have you been saying your seven?"

My silence told her the answer.

"I suppose they can wait," she said. "For now, you must get something good in you. I will tolerate no foolishness."

To my consternation I was unable to resist. She sat and, taking my head into her lap, fed me sips of pot liquor. The liquid was as savory as it was nourishing. I tasted essence of carrots and greens and marrow.

"Silent Mary brewed this just for you," she said.

I tried to speak but she hushed me.

"Just rest. And listen."

"Once upon a time in a kingdom by the sea," she began.

I closed my eyes again and felt the knots and twists in my body begin to ease. Pandora's stories, full of fairies and fortunes and gilded carriages, were completely unfamiliar. Yet, as I drifted off to sleep, I found comfort in believing they had been composed just for me.

Others at Placid Hall took turns keeping watch over me through the night and the following day. Silent Mary contributed her brooding presence. Milton, still lame from his wounded foot, drew pictures in the dirt while chattering without pause. Double Sam argued with his invisible brother. At the time I was uncertain of the precise nature of these visits, whether they actually took place or sprung from my fractured imagination. Only later was I able to confirm my friends' efforts to provide relief during my ordeal. An additional encounter, like Isaac's spectral visit, remained inexplicable. On my third and final night chained to the post, a remarkable sighting influenced my fate in ways too numerous to tally.

Rain had been falling for hours. Perhaps *fall* is too gentle a word. It was the kind of downpour that leaves scars, grooves, and dents in the earth. I shivered in my chains, blinking rapidly as it came down in sheets and pellets. With Silent Mary's broth coursing through my innards, I had regained sufficient strength to hold myself in a sitting position, resting my head against the post. I had only to be alive until daybreak and Greene would remove my chains, leaving me bound to him nonetheless.

Soaked to the bone, I awaited the dawn while considering the looming paradox of my situation. What little I had to live for.

In the distance, the splintered gray boards of our cabins appeared to tremble and dissolve in the wet. The resulting cloud of grayness, murky and unsettled, gradually took on new shapes, outlines of boys and girls. Struck dumb, I watched while they marched down the corridor of the quarters toward me before veering sharply and proceeding toward the plantation borders. Clad in garments I had never seen—nothing like our sackcloth and threadbare castoffs—they passed me in shades of gray, nearly close enough to touch. I had thought of my Ancestors as ancient, with a history of torment etched on their weathered faces. But these were children, ranging in age from five harvests to fifteen, with gleaming faces and vigorous frames. I didn't understand their youthfulness. I understood only that they had been in the world before I came to it, and that they now belonged to some other place. Occasionally a boy or girl would pause and look at me, then rejoin the procession without missing a step. They walked unsullied through the mud, as smoothly as if they were gliding on cushions of air. I called to them, but any sound I made was lost in the fury of the gale.

Already shivering, I became consumed by a different kind of chill, a peculiar sensation unlike anything I had ever known. I sensed the presence of an energy at work, quick, elusive, and beyond my comprehension. I did infer, however, that submitting to melancholy would undo the labors of those who had come before me, that I had an obligation to resist instead of giving in. I rose unsteadily to my feet, aware of my shackles but determined to somehow overcome them. My ancestors, so resolute and curiously young, had shown me a glimpse, perhaps, of the end of sorrows.

The last pilgrim in the strange parade lagged behind the others, growing taller as he approached. It was Isaac, grinning confidently.

"Mind yourself," he said, "and follow their footsteps."

"I'm trying," I shouted. "I'm trying!"

Isaac and the ghostly train disappeared into the fog. I strained against my chains, bellowing into the wind and rain until I passed out.

In the morning, I opened my eyes and saw the lovely face of my Pandora, preparing to revive me with a kiss.

Pandora

I came at sunrise with more of Silent Mary's pot liquor. Cato was sleeping, as I expected. But his body was oddly relaxed, much changed from his previous posture. He was smiling too, as if enveloped in a fanciful dream. He met my kiss with equal, steady pressure, and when he spoke his voice was clear and resonant. I knew at once that it was his old voice, the one whose absence he had often lamented. He told me that his ordeal was over, that there was nothing in this world strong enough to keep him down. He talked of Ancestors and an old friend named Isaac. Cradling his head in my hands, I pressed my face to his. Before, even as I was drawn to his gentle manner and his wonderful hands, I had harbored doubts about the weight he struggled under. I questioned how much of it I could pile onto my own shoulders. As I knelt beside him absorbing the signs of his renewal, my uncertainties melted away in the warm glow of morning. I knew then that we could carry each other.

III

Seraph

Little Zander had seen Nila beaten and banished, Cato nearly ruined. Cato had survived, Cupid was likely gone for good, and the world continued to make no sense. Now it was the still of the night and Zander hoped to elude the riddles that had fastened him to earth for days. He could practice his lifts and landings, flip and tumble as freely as he pleased. Whirling across the ground, he set loose the impulses that charged through him every minute of every day. He recognized he was born that way, filled with a zest that not even captivity could thwart. Temporarily free of his rock-crushing routine and the amused tolerance of his fellow Stolen, he could rise above the hateful jumble of Placid Hall, climb the sky as his mind and body merged, floating or zooming (the choice was his) until the treetops and cabins, water trough, and whipping post were as small as ants.

But first he had to reach the proper speed, a process that required preparation. In the serenity of the clearing he lunged forward with one leg, then the other, flexing and shaking his arms, when he heard the flap of wings. Then he saw the Buba Yali, crouched on a branch in the nearby woods. He had detected his presence before, felt his buzzing energy overhead, but he had never laid eyes on him in the flesh. Were angels made of flesh? He hadn't thought so. Yet the angel seemed composed of solid stuff. He wore an oversize coat that must have flapped when he moved through the trees. His hat was pulled low over his face and he had a pouch sack strung across one shoulder. Zander was swift of foot, perhaps faster than any man at Placid Hall, but the angel was faster. He scurried across tree branches as if they were solid ground, then landed softly as a whisper. It was then that Zander thought of Swing Low, the mysterious rescuer mentioned only in hushed tones, whose speed and grace were legendary. Moving with care, he trailed the Buba Yali deep into the woods, where the stream that ran through Placid Hall formed a small pool before trickling toward the neighboring farm. From behind a massive oak, he watched as the angel removed his boots, trousers, and, finally, his pouch, coat, and shirt. Later, back in the quarters, Zander would turn the encounter over and over in his mind, always returning to three details. First, the Buba Yali's back, marked exactly like his own, with six circular indentations in two evenly spaced vertical lines. Second, the shape of the body as the Buba Yali entered the water, the waist narrowing above hips that flared into entrancing curves. Third, the lovely slope of the Buba Yali's breasts when she rose and turned toward him, liquid gleaming on the downy triangle between her thighs. Swing Low was a woman, and she was smiling at him. How long had she known he was following her? Could she be smiling at someone else? Questions were still forming when someone crept behind him and clapped a hand over his mouth.

IV

The Entire Bountiful World

William

As far as we could tell, Greene had given up trying to solve the mystery of Cupid's vanishing. His rock-crushing operation was missing three men. Besides Cupid, Cato was still recovering and Milton's foot continued to hobble him. Greene brought two Stolen from Pleasant Grove to supplement our crew. Ben was a tall, heavy-lidded fellow who spoke slowly and seemed to think in the same manner. He seldom answered questions directly, and words fell oddly from his tongue. Clarence was a stocky, talkative man with a quick temper and yellow teeth. Two months after joining us, they hadn't yet earned our trust and seemed in no hurry to obtain it. Supervising them was part of my tasks in my new role at Placid Hall.

We had seen little of Greene during Cato's sufferings at the whipping post. After our cabinmate's survival seemed assured, Greene summoned me to the pit. Dormant while the men and I had been busy with other tasks, Cannonball's Folly was cast in shadows that we never noticed while turning the great wheel. Boulders piled at the bottoms of the chutes. The iron auger hovered above the center of the pit, its oak arms poised to revolve.

Greene stood with his hands on his hips, studying the machinery while he awaited my approach. Pandora, three paces behind him, held his book of notes.

"Billy Boy," he said, "you're my new foreman."

"Yassuh. Why me, suh?"

"Because you're a creature that respects its limitations. I'm not just an astute judge of human nature. I have substantial knowledge of nigga behavior as well. When my book on the subject is published everyone will come to rely on my expertise. I will have to alter my schedule to allow for all the lectures I'll be asked to give. Most men would be daunted by the responsibilities I already have, managing my lands, managing all of you. But I realize that my Creator expects more of me, which is why he has blessed me with so many enviable qualities. While I won't overtax you by requiring you to think beyond your capacities, I may find myself depending on you to lead the crew more often in days to come. You may not fully believe that you're up to the task. But I wouldn't call upon you if I doubted your readiness. You understand me, Billy Boy?"

I had foreseen just such a conversation. I no more wanted to lead Greene's crew than I wanted to stick my head in a cluster of nettles. Still, I understood that neither Cato nor Milton was equipped to take on the task, and Double Sam too distracted. Ben and Clarence, being new, could hardly be expected to lead. While Greene prattled on, I began to consider what I could gain. Perhaps I could shape the schedule and the labor to make our lives more tolerable while keeping Greene unaware. I would have more time for Margaret, Cato could see more of Pandora. Zander would have more time to practice flying. Double Sam could bicker with his brother. And the new men could conspire together, as was their habit.

"You respect me, William," Greene was saying, "and the other niggas respect you. You will do what I tell you, and they will do what you tell them. That's the beauty of the system."

I nodded slowly, as if finally catching the meaning of his words. "What if Cupid come back? What if he git found?"

Greene turned away. I almost thought I saw a tear forming in the corner of his eye. "Well, you let me be concerned about that. Gather the niggas tonight and tell them they'll resume their regimen in the morning."

"Yassuh," I said. "'Spectfully, suh, Ah needs ta ax ya sumthin'. When Cupid was fo'man, ya lets 'im keep Nila in his cabin. Ah'd sho' be pleased to have Margrit in mine."

Greene looked amused. "I expect you'll also want his wine gourd."

"Thank you kindly, boss," I said, scratching my head. "But Margrit will do."

"Well, look at you, a negotiating nigga. I will have her fetched from Two Forks as soon as Holtzclaw can spare her. I suppose she can wash linens as well as Nila did."

We returned to the pit the following day and found the stones just as stubborn as they had always been. True to his word, Greene watched us less often as spring stretched into summer. Pandora reported that he was busy preparing his book and entertaining the idea of running for something called the Senate. But he maintained his usual intensity when he did come around, scribbling notes and waiting to inspect us at the end of the day. While Cato had somehow come back with renewed vigor and confidence, Milton never regained full strength. He limped often and some days had to refrain from labor entirely. Meanwhile, Zander became as fiddle-footed as a bandit. And he had seldom been steady to begin with.

Ransom

I loved her, of course. She loved me too, would tell me so from time to time. As much as that pleased me, I realized even then that love perhaps meant something different to her, and if by chance it didn't, her love was more powerful than mine. One touch from an extraordinary woman like her was all it took to inspire in me a vision of a far simpler, safer life. Like her, like everyone in our secret league, I'd dedicated my life to defeating Thievery. Yet she only had to say the word and I would have forsaken the spying, masquerades, and death-defying errands that our calling required. In contrast, her fidelity to the mission ranked above all things.

We met on the Chariot, the name I will give to the network of allies who helped Stolen escape from bondage. We avoided real names to minimize the consequences should a conspirator be captured and forced to disclose all she knew. I was a daylight agent. With my priestly garb and my handy Book, I could move in and out of Thievery territory mostly unmolested. Because furtiveness was her specialty, she traveled principally by night and was careful to gather no moss. As soon as she sealed an arrangement or transferred a passenger, she was gone, into the shadows. After a number of successful exchanges over a succession of years, trust grew inevitably between us. It surprised neither of us when it bloomed into something more. She called me Preacher Man. Like everyone else I called her Swing Low.

She knew that I could hold my tongue in the midst of arguments in the quarters, where Stolen debated whether Swing Low was a demon or an angel, whether Swing Low existed at all. Some boasted of having seen "him" in the flesh, had sworn that he could make himself tall as a tree or small as a mouse. Others declared he could sneak up on a bear and topple it with a tickle. Some said he was an African prince or the president of Canada. Self-proclaimed witnesses said he had words he could mumble in a Thief's ear and send him to sleep forever. She knew I could stay silent no matter how tempted I was to brag or tell them the simple truth. She knew I could love her and keep it to myself.

Even now it seems improper to speak of her so openly. Even now it feels as if I've said too much.

Cato

After Milton had yet another rough day in the pit, he suggested we lay hands on him. We could ask our Ancestors to make him whole, he said, and enable him to get to Two Forks and see his family. Zander and I quickly consented. Even Ben and Clarence went along with our effort, supposing it couldn't hurt. I went to Cupid's old cabin, where William had begun to settle in, and invited him to join us.

He was inclined on the rope bed, idly rubbing one of Margaret's kerchiefs against his cheek.

"You could say some words," I said.

He snorted. "Might as well say to them to the air. Milton will get better or he won't."

"You talked me out of my despair, William. You refused to let me die. That's how I know you believe in something. Milton and Zander don't think so, but I know better."

He sat up sideways on the bed, his feet on the hard dirt floor. "Why is everybody always concerned about what I believe?"

I moved to the center of the room, pretending to straighten the cup and plate on his table. "You're a curiosity. You stood up to a runaway horse. You stood up to Cupid."

"You stood up to him too," he said.

"It wasn't the same. People think you'll stand up to anything. We suspect you do for it a reason. You must have a notion that there's something after this."

"Why should anyone take heed to what I think about what happens next? *This* is enough for me. This life. When this is over I want *everything* to be over. No next. I'm not saying it's what I believe. I'm saying it's what I want."

"When this is over I want everything to be just beginning," I told him. "A whole other life waiting for us."

"What if it's this all over again? One life is enough."

"That sounds like punishment," I said.

"Could it be any worse than what's already happened to you? What if it's exactly the same? More Thieves. More Cupids. I've already had more of them than I can bear."

It was my turn to snort. "Hardly," I said. "You have no idea what you can bear. I just want to belong to myself. To feel what that's like."

"What would you call a Stolen who's no longer stolen?"

"Just free, I suppose."

William rose, moved past me, and stood in the doorway of the cabin. I wondered if he was eager for me to leave. "How do we even know there's such a thing as free people like us? I mean, really free. Have you ever seen one?"

"I see Ransom. He seems real enough."

He frowned and folded his arms across his chest. "The Thieves let him walk around like he's pale as a fish belly. Tell me that doesn't seem strange to you."

I shrugged, but he didn't see me. "He has papers," I said.

"Where did he get them?"

"He says there's a place full of people like us and none of them are Stolen."

"Heaven. I'm sick of hearing of it. Angels, all that."

"No, that's not what I mean. He talks about it in the clearing after he's put their Book away. After the circling and shouting too. When there's just a few listeners left, he tells us about another place. He says if you don't believe in it you'll never find it."

"That makes no sense."

"It makes perfect sense to me."

"Why all of a sudden are you so certain?"

I didn't tell him about the children marching past me in the rain, about Isaac's advice to follow in their footsteps. To never quit. I hadn't even told Pandora that I had seen Ancestors with my own eyes, and in so doing had renewed my faith. Coming down to the quarters one day after my strength returned, I saw William and the others staring at marks on the ground. They thought that hailstones had made them. I knew they were footprints.

"Because certainty is strength," I replied. "You once reminded me that we come from Strong. Now I'm reminding you."

Ransom

When the boy saw Swing Low waiting for me in the water, I pressed my hand over his mouth and dragged him into the shadows.

"You don't belong here," I told him. "Get back to the quarters."

"I just want to know about her wings," Zander said. "I saw her back."

I knew he had seen much more than that.

"I also saw her flying, Preacher. Riding the air from tree to tree. I want to do that."

"Not tonight, Zander. It's too dangerous to talk about this now."

"If it's so dangerous, Preacher, what are you doing here?"

I looked into the boy's eyes and thought I saw his future. Hadn't Swing Low spoken of a new army rising from the glorious youth, the best of our children? He was nimble, alert, and nearly glowed with a restless intelligence. Anyone could see it.

"I am on an errand of critical importance, a task that must remain undisclosed. I am trusting you to keep my secret."

He nodded. "I won't tell anyone," he said. "But the marks on her back. Can you at least tell me about them? If you won't, maybe she will."

"You will hear all you need to know but not at the present. If you want to be a Buba Yali yourself, you mustn't rush things. You have to bide your time."

I took his elbow and escorted him a few paces in the direction of the quarters. I said he was not yet ready to parley with seraphim, that I would eventually share certain confidences with him. Little by little, I told him, he would learn to take flight.

Cato

Milton had replaced his drawing stick with a walking stick, fashioned from a branch Little Zander had fetched for him. He used it when he wasn't at the pit. William assigned him to sweep out the rock dust, to keep sticks and impurities out of the machinery. The task was usually Zander's. With Milton hobbled it became a convenient way to provide him respite from the wheel. As soon as the day's labor ended, he would throw himself down on the stoop of our cabin and yank off his boots. Each time, his injured foot emerged swollen and mottled. His initial wound, despite various treatments, never seemed to close completely. Redness inevitably seeped through the rags tied around it.

Greene concluded one work session prematurely, when there were still several hours of daylight left. He summoned Milton to the rear of the big house where, Pandora reported, he was laid in the bed of a cart. At first we feared that he was going to be sold. But Pandora, having spotted Dr. LeMaire on the premises, speculated that he was likely seeing to Milton's injury. We were heartened to learn that Greene was getting Milton the care he needed—until William reckoned he was just protecting his investment. I couldn't help recalling the time Greene warned William that he was not as costly as he supposed. Any of us could be replaced at any time, sold or traded for seeds or trinkets. Screech Owl had once exchanged one of her husband's favorite housemaids for a bundle of rare Parisian silks. Greene did not approve, but I'm certain he understood her impulse. In a pinch, he would put us in his pocket quick.

Our corner of the quarters included a pair of long, low benches flanking a crude, rough-hewn table. Here and there stood sections of tree trunk that served as both stool and counters, depending on the need. We were gathered there when Milton returned, his limp as pronounced as ever. We were amusing ourselves with a game of seeds and pits, a contest in which the players moved seeds in and out of holes dug into a board. Cupid had discouraged us from playing because he lacked the patience and strategy needed to capture an opponent's seeds. With him gone we had taken to it eagerly. Our new crew members, Ben and Clarence, had played often at Pleasant Grove and were highly skilled compared to the rest of us. William, Zander, and I watched as they matched wits, trading insults as they played.

We briefly turned our attention to Milton as he slumped heavily to our stoop and pushed off his boots. He dabbed at his mouth with a bloody scrap of cloth before rising and, leaning hard on his stick, made his way over to us.

"You're bleeding at both ends," Clarence observed.

"I know," Milton said.

We demanded to know what had happened.

"Traded Greene three of my teeth," Milton explained.

"Traded them for what?" William asked.

"Lost time. He said I owed him for all the days I've missed."

"What does he need your teeth for?" Zander asked, relinquishing his seat so that Milton could stretch his leg and rest his wounded foot on the stump.

He nodded at Zander in appreciation before answering. "He's going to put them in his own mouth, of course, just like George Washington. I'll get along without them." Milton pressed the rag to his lips, then folded it in his hand. "They were back teeth. Their absence will do no harm to my charming smile."

"We'll let Sarah be the judge of that," William said.

The mention of Sarah's name seemed to slow Milton's thoughts for a moment. "It's been so long since I've seen her."

"How will you manage to eat?" Zander asked.

"As if bone soup needed much chewing," Milton replied.

"Don't sound like a good trade," Clarence said, without looking up from the game.

"Don't remember asking you," Milton said.

"I sold two of my teeth to my old Thief," Clarence countered. "I got coins for my troubles. But you got nothing you can touch or hold on to."

"I can hold on to my hide," Milton said. "I'd rather Greene takes it out of my mouth than out of my back."

Clarence signaled his disapproval with a grunt. "He gets the better of it either way," he said.

"Don't fret, Milton," Zander said. "You'll be put right soon enough. You'll be walking as good as new. Then you'll be running, and you know what comes after that. Flying. Higher and higher, until you're close enough to kiss the stars."

Ben laughed. Whenever he laughed, Clarence laughed with him.

"You won't be thinking about stars so much after you've kissed a woman," Ben said.

"Leave him be," William said. "He's got time for that."

Ben shook his head. "Strange thing to ever tell a Stolen he's got time."

"That boy's still got sugar tit on his breath," William said. "Just a baby and should stay that way awhile before he starts making babies of his own. Once that starts there's no going back."

"I'd rather put my babies down in the river than see a Thief get his claws in them," Clarence said.

Ben grunted and idly stroked himself. "I've made plenty of

babies, and I'm none the worse for it," he bragged. He turned to Zander. "You're about the right age. I might even be your pappy."

"Angels are not born of man," Zander said. "It says so in the Book."

"Live by Thieves' words and you are bound to die by them," William warned.

"There's no other way to die," Ben said. He turned and spat into the dust.

Clarence fixed his eyes on me. "How about you, Cato? You must have made some children."

"None that I know of. I wanted to, with Iris. Well, after her I figured I was done with all of that."

Ben laughed again. "Guess when I'll be done with all of that," he said. "When I'm dead."

Clarence would not let the subject go. "I think you've changed your mind, Cato," he said. "You saw Pandora and everything changed."

"That's some good stuff right there," Ben said. "I can tell."

It was true that Pandora and I had become quite close. But I have never been comfortable talking about such things. "You speculate," I said to Clarence, "but you don't know."

He laughed. "We might be Stolen, Cato, but we're not blind."

"She is pleasing to my eye, I'll allow. It's mainly her stories I like. When Greene had me chained to the post, she came and told me fables about strange, enchanted places."

"Stories and fables," Milton chirped. "Most men call them breasts and backsides."

"No," Ben said. "Real men call them bubbies and cunts."

I found Ben easy to ignore. So did William. I could tell that talk of children had disturbed him. I wondered if he'd finally gotten Margaret bigged.

"Milton," William said, "so how exactly do your teeth get into Greene's mouth?"

"LeMaire is going to do it. Hardly felt it when he took mine out."

"Liar," Clarence said.

"No, I mean it," Milton said. "I just sang my grandmother's song. Gets me through anything."

Ignoring his pain, he hummed a fragment of the song and shook his one good foot to the rhythm. Milton had been a nimble dancer. He could perform the Thieves' jigs and reels as stiffly as they. He could twist and jump through a ring shout or slide to the beat of soles tapping on the earth. He danced with every woman he could, although he loved only Sarah. He claimed he had learned to dance from his grandmother. One might think we were all tired of his grandmother stories. He had so many that we privately wondered whether he had imagined them all. It was rare for a Stolen to know a grandparent so well. According to Milton's account, his grandmother would put his tiny feet on top of hers and allow him to whisk her around their cabin. Listening to him, we found ourselves inside those memories, whirling with the two of them, knowing the softness and scents of maternal love. Whirling and twirling until we were tired and ready for sleep. One by one we retired to our cabins until only Milton remained, sitting on the stoop. Holding the rag to his mouth and looking up at the stars.

Margaret

Four walls. Two plates, two cups. A table, two chairs. A bed.
Some Stolen tried to improve the look of their cabins, make
some beauty from whatever scraps they could find. William had
done nothing to the place we were going to share besides sweep the
dirt floor. The only bright thing was the grin he was wearing when
I stepped off the supply wagon and into his arms. Perhaps he was
leaving the decorating to me.

In the cabin, I returned his kisses until I felt his hands sliding
my dress above my hips. I pushed him away.

"That has to come down," I told him.

"What?"

"That rope bed. Take it down."

"But I've been lying on it."

"You won't be lying on it with me."

"Why?"

"Do you really need to ask? Cupid and Nila were in that bed.
He hurt her in it."

William looked at the bed as if he hadn't seen it before. He
blinked like he was newly born and the light hurt his eyes.

"Margaret, where in Greene's kingdom has a Stolen escaped

being hurt? Every rock, every blossom, every blade of grass has our blood on it."

"But you won't be loving me on those rocks. I won't be clutching you in that grass, holding on to you, trying to keep you moving inside me instead of pulling away. That will happen in here. And it won't happen on that bed."

William stared at the bed, his hands on his hips. He let out a long breath, so much air escaping him that I thought he might collapse.

"A lot of trouble to gather shucks and make a new pallet," he said.

"I suppose you'll find me worthy."

"I didn't mean it like that."

"How did you mean it, then?"

He gave up, and after throwing his hands in the air he moved to the bed and began to take it apart.

My mood had spoiled. Since Greene had given his permission for me to move to Placid Hall, I had spent nearly every minute consumed by thoughts of William, of spending the entire night with him, of waking up after long loving with him still beside me. Now that the time had come, it was furthest from my mind.

William

We spent the night on the pallet I had quickly assembled. It was not very long or wide, yet Margaret somehow managed to put considerable space between us. She turned her back to me and hardly stirred. I, on the other hand, twitched and fiddled, unable to sleep. After what felt like hours of restlessness, I rose and left the cabin.

I knocked at Guinea Jack's door, and, for the first time, he asked who was there. I wondered at this change, since it was unlikely that anyone other than myself ever visited him at such an unusual hour. I took his grunt for a welcome and entered his hut. He neither rose nor spoke when I approached his table.

"Good evening," I said. "I find myself wanting some of your special tea."

"Shouldn't you be having tea with your mate?"

"Margaret's not in the mood for tea. Or anything else."

I waited for Guinea Jack to invite me to sit. He made no such offer.

"Understandable," he said. "The man she loves is not the man she's come to be with."

"Nonsense," I said. "What does that even mean?"

"She loves William. Not some twisted version of him."

Guinea Jack had always spoken his mind. But that night his words contained a goodly measure of venom, more than enough of it to sting. I squinted at him, though a single candle provided all the light in the hut. "That's not—What are you saying?"

"I'm being quite clear." He got up and poured one cup of tea. After blowing carefully on its surface, he looked up at me. "You sleep in Cupid's cabin, you oversee your brethren for crumbs from a Thief's table. Have you flayed a Stolen yet?"

"I have not, and I won't, ever. Can you blame me for wanting to live a little better, for wanting to have my woman beside me? No more night walking for me. No more dodging paddy rollers just to be with Margaret for a few precious minutes before hurrying back here before dawn. No more risking an injury that refuses to heal. Talk to Milton, he knows what I mean. That's all I'm doing it for."

"And at what price?"

"Could the price be any steeper than what I've paid? What we all pay? What would you have me do?"

He sipped from his tea. "Listen to yourself talking in circles. You're just about ruined. You're doing exactly what the Thief wants you to do, to forget who the real enemy is and do his sordid work for him—and now you're being rewarded with wine and women. You're no better than Cupid. He had blood in his eye. At least he had an excuse."

My knees buckled as if the old man had walloped me. Head pounding, eyes watering, I cried out in protest. "Guinea Jack, you're not being fair," I said. "Please, hear me out."

He said nothing as he walked to the door and opened it. "As long as you're that Thief's lackey, you're not welcome here."

I staggered to the door in a fog, but then he reached out a hand and stopped me. I sighed, thinking he had changed his mind. Instead he went to the table beside his bed and returned with his two carved figurines, Mother and Father Root.

"Here," he said. "You need these more than I do."

Cato

Even after three months at Placid Hall, Clarence had only Ben to claim as a friend. They whispered confidences and shared amusements and on some days tolerated the rest of us with barely concealed disdain. Ben was quiet, a most fortunate disposition, except on the subject of women. He boasted of his conquests with such detail and enthusiasm that I suspected most of them were imaginary. Clarence, in contrast, was seldom silent. His garrulousness was exceeded only by his odor, which closely resembled onions gone to rot.

"Why is that nigga always running and jumping?" he asked one evening as dusk settled.

There were other Stolen who referred to their brethren by that hateful name. Cupid had. However, Clarence was the only one with whom I was forced to keep company.

"His name is Zander, as you know," I sputtered. "He's practicing flying."

The boy was up to his usual activity, spreading wide his arms and dashing to and fro.

"He's what?"

"Zander practices flying on nights when the moon is bright," I explained with more than typical zest. I somehow felt that by insulting Zander, Clarence was also insulting me. "He says he's learning to steer by the stars."

Clarence laughed so hard he nearly succumbed from a fit of choking. I later described our exchange to William, whose lack of concern perturbed me.

"What do you expect me to do about it?" William asked.

"Something," I said. "You're the foreman. It's your job."

"I'll thank you to do your own job, not mine," he said. "I'll tolerate him as long as he does his work. I'm not Cupid. I get no pleasure from bringing pain."

I don't know exactly what I wanted William to do. Perhaps I'd convinced myself that a stern discussion with Clarence would suffice to correct his behavior. Or perhaps I was unsure that my misgivings about his character were actually of substance and not merely a case of our personalities conflicting. In any case, William was too preoccupied with his own troubles to be of much help.

If we could have foreseen the extent of Clarence's mischief and the consequences it would eventually produce, I have no doubt we would have acted to prevent it.

One morning in the pit, Milton was struggling terribly. With his bad foot, he couldn't keep pace with our turning of the wheel, and no adjustment we made improved our situation until William put him on sweep duty again. He probably should have been left in our cabin to rest, but Greene had insisted that he earn his keep. Instead of encouraging our ailing brother, Clarence commenced to goading Milton as he swept. He whispered rumors he claimed to have heard about Holtzclaw and Sarah, distracting Milton such that he stumbled in front of the wheel, directly in the path of a revolving spoke. He took a crushing blow to the head and fell to the ground. William halted work and we brought him back to the quarters. We didn't expect him to survive the night.

Margaret

Milton's mouth was so swollen that we couldn't even get water or broth past his lips. Silent Mary, despite having seen many illnesses, examined him and came away with no solution. Trusting Pandora to mind the food being prepared for Greene's lunch table, she stirred herbs in a dented kettle until clouds of steam rose up around her broad face. She strained the resulting liquid through a cloth that she folded and placed in a basket with several others. Following her instructions, I laid the damp bandages across Milton's brow, returning periodically for more. Mary made it clear that her efforts were only intended to ease Milton's suffering. She could do little beyond that. I was going back to the laundry station to resume my task of washing and boiling linens when the supply wagon arrived with provisions for Mary's larder. The driver hopped off and commenced unloading sacks of flour, sugar, and salt.

Sarah slid out from under the tarp he had unfolded. Her hair was a sweaty tangle slipping loose from her kerchief. Dark rings circled her eyes. Worry rode her hard. She marched toward me, and I took her hand in mine.

"Sarah," I said. "Whatever possessed you—?"

"It was the fastest way."

The Entire Bountiful World

"But you'll have to go back on foot. You'll never make it back to Two Forks before you're missed. You won't even get back before nightfall. There will be trouble for certain."

She shrugged and straightened her sackcloth dress. "I'll take the beating. I had to come. Take me to him."

"Who told you?"

"Nobody told me. I just felt it. Take me to him."

"Your baby. Where is she?"

"With Nila," she hissed, pushing past me. "Now, no more questions, Margaret. Take me to him."

Milton was flat on his back in his cabin. His bandage had somehow slid down over his eyes. Breathing had become a soft, labored whistling. Sarah nursed him as hours passed, dabbing at his brow and the corners of his mouth, leaning over him to whisper in his ear. I watched from the doorway as she removed her kerchief and dipped it in the moist hollows of his neck and collarbones. She pressed it to her nose before tucking it between her breasts. When Milton's faint gasping gave way to a troubling rattle, she held his hand in hers and offered her goodbye. She was kissing him on his forehead when I went out and sat on the stoop. Soon humming commenced, a deep sound expressing a sorrow big enough to take us all in, bigger than the words that followed.

No more auction block for me,
No more, no more.
No more auction block for me,
Many thousands gone.

No more pint of salt for me,
No more, no more.

Yonder

No more pint of salt for me,
Many thousands gone.

Sarah's voice was not lovely, but it was strong. It never wavered as she sang him home.

Cato

Although it often looked as if we approached our tasks with passion, our hearts were never in our work. More often than not, we labored with a certain dispatch because it kept our minds on our duties. Remaining alert protected our bodies, reduced the chance of a crushed limb or smashed nose brought on by carelessness. Exertion distracted us from the slow tread of time that did not belong to us. We worked while thinking of other things, fully aware that our private thoughts were our most precious possession. With Milton on our minds, we had resumed our toil with considerably less pace.

Returning from the pit, we saw Margaret standing in the path leading to the quarters, her arms folded against her chest. When we got closer, she shook her head to let us know that Milton had died. Soon we heard wailing. In the doorway of our cabin, Sarah sobbed in Silent Mary's arms.

Little Zander had been leading the way. He stopped in his tracks, stumbling a little as he took in the scene. After staring at the ground for a long minute, he wiped his eyes with his fists, like a little child mustering the strength to bawl. Then he lifted his chin.

"It's all right," he said. "Milton's dancing with his grandmother now."

Behind him, Ben scratched himself and snorted. "Fuck dancing with an old wench," he said. "When I get to heaven I'm dancing with whores. One on each arm."

We paused and turned toward Ben, each of us staring at him in disbelief.

"That's presuming a lot," I said.

Ben returned my retort with a grin, moving so close to me that his overlong nose hairs appeared to sprout as he spoke. "Pussy above and pussy below," he chanted. "Some pussy's fast and some pussy's slow. Pussy below and pussy above. Pussy in the sky is the kind I love. Cato, your face tells me you think I ain't going to heaven."

"On the contrary. I'm thinking about how fast we can get you there."

"Is that right?" Ben shoved me hard, knocking me into Double Sam. We both stayed on our feet.

"I swear it on my seven words," I replied, shoving him back.

We began the familiar shuffle with fists raised.

"No," I heard William say. "Wrong time. Wrong place."

But he was too late. Ben no longer sounded like himself. Nor did he look like himself. In the waning light he had become a different foe altogether, one I was determined to prevent from haunting me. Soon, I knew, he would be teasing me about the woman I loved. Not much later, I was certain, he'd be raising his foot above my throat. I had to act fast. I surprised him by leaving my feet and leaping onto him, knocking him on his back. I saw terror in his eyes as I seized his throat with both hands.

"I've had enough, Cupid," I said, sucking my teeth. "No more!"

William grabbed me from behind and wrestled me away.

"Mind yourself, Cato," he warned. "Ben! Ben! Stay where you are!"

William called his name twice to bring me back to the present.

To remind me where I was, that Cupid was dead. I nodded to show him I understood.

Ben, gasping, rose to a sitting position. He tried to look amused, but I wasn't fooled. He was frightened. Double Sam went and stood near him but made no move to help him. Ben gave no indication that he'd heard me call him Cupid.

"I would have had you, Cato," he said. "Thank your friend William for coming to save you."

William cocked his head at Ben, smiling just a little. "Be assured. You are the one I'm saving."

That night, William and I found ourselves again sharing the work of digging a grave. Sarah and Silent Mary had washed Milton's body and prepared it for burial in the morning. We agreed that Ben and Clarence were best left to their own devices. Double Sam had been enlisted to aid the delivery of a calf, and Little Zander had been too forlorn to do us much good. We toiled in Hush Harbor, the portion of Placid Hall where Stolen were laid to rest. The moon was timid, giving us only a weak light that we supplemented with a pair of homemade torches stuck in the ground at an opportune distance. With the bones of the fallen surrounding me, my thoughts wandered quite naturally to my fateful encounter with the Ancestors. I considered that they might choose to visit me once more, in environs so familiar to them. But I saw no sign. if they were watching, they gave no indication. Aside from the peeps and warbling of unseen creatures, there were few noises beyond the sound of our spades plunging into the soil. At first we worked without speaking, until William broke the silence.

"Brothers should be able to talk freely with each other," he said. "Speak your mind."

"All right," I said. "If you had disciplined Clarence when I suggested it, Milton might still be alive."

William stopped digging and wiped his brow with the end of his shirt. "I could say the same about your thoughts and prayers. When you all pressed palms to his flesh and mumbled your magic words. Did Milton feel any better the next day? Did he suddenly stop limping? Perhaps if you and the others had mumbled a little louder, maybe all would be well."

He leaned on his spade, waiting. I had no answer for him, so I said nothing and kept digging. "Cato, what if I hadn't stopped you and Ben? What if I had let you go at it?"

I tossed away a clump of earth. Adopting a posture similar to William's, I said, "Then we'd be digging two graves instead of one. Or my body would be waiting to join Milton's in the ground."

"I'm your brother, remember? I would not have allowed that to happen."

"I don't know about that. I think Clarence would have kept you at bay until Ben got the best of me."

William laughed, a quick, explosive response that surprised me. "I'm not afraid of Clarence," he said. "Pandora, on the other hand. I do fear her wrath. Woe betide the man who brings her bad news."

He grinned and I grinned back. Then we remembered our grim duty, and melancholy promptly replaced our brief merriment. We pitched into the earth as if our friend was already underneath it and only our efforts could raise him from the clammy depths.

Pandora

The girl Calliope stood under Screech Owl's window. In some peculiar spell of mercy, Greene's wife had allowed her to rest the slop jar atop her head on a kerchief instead of holding it aloft with arms outstretched as she had commanded me. Calliope stood silently, waiting, I supposed, for the harsh call of her mistress, the signal to turn the jar upon herself. Yet I also wondered if perhaps Screech Owl spared her that indignity, deeming her too young to offer unwitting competition for Greene's wandering eyes. There was also the matter of her face, nearly ruined by the pitcher that Screech Owl had broken across her lovely features. The scar ran from hairline to chin, pulsing redly across her purple blackness. In years to come when I would think of her, an image of a dark plum would enter my mind, with a burning ember at its core instead of a pit. I encountered Calliope soon after Greene summoned us to the yard on the morning after Milton's passing.

Speaking from his porch, he encouraged us to reflect upon the death as an opportunity to ponder the rightful path to a glorious hereafter. There, he promised, the most virtuous of us could enjoy an eternal reward as servants attending our Creator's needs. It was a speech we'd heard before but I had doubts that Greene would be able to complete it that morning. During my time with him, I became so accustomed to his habits and bearing that I could immediately recognize the signs of his discomfort. He would pause for long periods between sentences, for example, and rub his belly with both hands as he spoke. He did each of those then, leading me to suspect that his breakfast or perhaps his supper the night before had not settled well in him. About five sentences into his address, his face turned a florid red and he abruptly stopped, turned, and hurried inside. We waited, some of us chattering quietly, others swaying on their feet and struggling to remain awake, until he returned, looking frail but somewhat adjusted. He resumed his speech, but once again he had to suddenly abandon it as he bolted indoors for relief. The murmurs among us rose to something bolder in his absence, and I took the opportunity to stroll briefly about the yard. My ramblings led me to Calliope.

Flies swirled about her in thick clouds, crawling over her with such abandon that I considered the possibility that she had died standing up, until she blinked dully amid the buzzing swarm. Between her feet, an equally busy gathering of insects revealed that the girl had soiled herself and the ground. It required all my resolve to approach her.

"What happened, child?"

She started to speak but first had to spit and repel the most enterprising of the flies, who saw her parted lips as a fresh opportunity. "I h-h-helped m-myself to . . . b-biscuits," she replied.

She must have known that we were allowed to consume Silent Mary's biscuits only on special occasions. Otherwise they were meant solely for Greene, his family, and his guests. I later learned that Screech Owl had been starving Calliope in hopes of delaying her development of the womanly curves her husband found so enticing. At the time, I attributed the girl's transgression to a combination of feeble wit and childish impudence. Still, I refrained from chastising her, knowing that the Greenes were far more liberal with admonishments than they were with food.

"Goodness' sake," I said. "That's just the kind of thing to do you harm."

"I know," she said, surprising me. "I was so hungry. One bite was all I took."

"How long have you been out here?"

"C-can't reckon."

Her teeth chattered despite the day's rising warmth, and she was nearly nonsensical with fatigue.

"Here," I said, "let me share your burden." I reached for the jar and barely settled my fingers around the handles when a piercing yell rang out above our heads. I stepped back and looked up to see Screech Owl glaring down at us from the window.

"Get away from her," she hissed.

Fearing I'd made things worse for Calliope, I patted her on the shoulder. "I'm sorry," I whispered, before returning to the front of the house, where the crowd waited for Greene to finish his speech.

William

At length Greene appeared on the porch once more. He had changed shirts and wiped as much sweat as he could from his hair and brow. Waiting until he had our full attention, he took a deep breath and advised us to trust Milton's soul to the almighty, a god who cradled the entire bountiful world in the palm of his hand. At almost the same time, Pandora rejoined us at the front of the house. But Greene was so disturbed by his rumbling bowels that he didn't notice her. He sighed and stared at his feet. He rubbed his belly and kept his head bowed for a long moment. Finally he looked up and spoke quickly.

"Clearly the Lord does not intend for me to speak today. You are dismissed. Put him under with haste."

Before we hurried off to bury Milton, Sarah approached the veranda. She stood at the bottom step but dared go no farther.

"Boss Greene," she said. "Boss Greene, suh."

He had collapsed into a chair and stretched out his legs. He didn't look strong enough to head inside, although he clearly needed to.

"Yes, what is it?"

"It's me, suh, Sarah."

"Yes, Sarah, what is it?"

"I'm much obliged to you for letting me be with Milton," she told him.

"It was a fruitful match," he said, closing his eyes.

"Boss Greene?"

"What now?"

"Kin Ah stay at Placid Hall until the homegoing tonight? I would sho' be thankful to hear Preacher Ransom."

"Now, Sarah, isn't it enough that I haven't had you skinned for being here in the first place? If I make an exception for you I'll have to start giving every nigga special treatment. Besides, Holtzclaw's come to fetch you."

Sarah's back was to us, so I couldn't see her face, but I imagine it had the same look of horror and surprise that I saw on Margaret's. Later we realized that she had hurried to Placid Hall because of two desires, to see Milton one last time and to escape Holtzclaw, who, informed of Milton's steady decline, had already made some arrangement with Greene to have his way with Sarah.

Margaret

Some hours after we laid Milton to rest, I waited with Sarah beside Holtzclaw's wagon. He usually sent a Stolen man on errands to Placid Hall, but he'd elected to drive the five miles himself. We watched him on the veranda, shaking hands with Greene. His other hand held a sack likely filled with bread and sweets from Greene's lunch table. When I hugged Sarah, something felt out of sorts; she was stiff in my arms and her expression was so blank that it troubled me. I had a feeling she might do something awful.

"Mind your step," I told her. "Between Greene and Holtzclaw—"

She eyed me curiously, lips curled in scorn. "You speaking for Greene now? He put you in charge?"

I almost asked her why she was so angry. But I didn't because of course I knew. "I'm trying to look out for you. You do right by Greene, he'll be more likely to do right by your child." I hated the words as they spilled from my mouth. But I didn't know what else to say.

Sarah laughed, a bitter sound. "My child."

"Yes, your *baby*. We whispered over her."

Sarah looked past me, her eyes on Holtzclaw as he swaggered toward us. "There are no babies around here, Margaret," she said.

"Just pickaninnies and bucks, young wenches, old wenches, and gray-headed boys. Nobody gets to be a baby."

I looked on in silence as Holtzclaw lifted Sarah into the rear of the wagon. I tried to meet her eyes one more time, but they were closed and her lips were pressed tight, as if she were avoiding a terrible stench. I remained in place as the wagon pulled away and down the path, shielding my eyes with my hand. To my disgust, Ben and Clarence appeared at my side, in the midst of some errand. They, too, watched Holtzclaw and Sarah fade from view.

"He could hardly wait until her man was in the ground," Clarence said.

Ben, far from a gentleman, stroked himself and spat. "I wouldn't tarry either," he said.

V
Haint

S arah had half a mind to stare at the sun while Holtzclaw hauled her back to Two Forks, to just gaze directly into it until she went blind. It was his fondest entertainment, holding the women's faces in place as he thrust away on top of them, forcing them to look into his eyes while he took his pleasure. Blind, she could claim a small, private victory, no matter how forcefully Holtzclaw gripped her skull. But then she considered the possibility that lack of sight might magnify other sensations: his abrasive touch, his pungent reek. Milton, Holtzclaw's opposite in every way, had been a kind and forgiving soul, and she had been glad to feel his warmth. As long as she drew breath she would savor the memory of his quick smile and nimble feet, his magnificent gift of picture making. She was at peace with his passing. His suffering was over, she had done right by him, and he had done more than right by her. She had known all along that it couldn't last. That nothing could.

The baby's color had never deepened. Sometimes it took days, weeks, for the darkness, pooled in buttocks and ears, to spread throughout the body. But Sarah's girl, pink as roses when she emerged, would never progress beyond a pale shade of beige. Though denizens of the quarters were hardly averse to gossip, they said little about the disparity between the girl's complexion and her parents' dark faces. It was not uncommon, after all, and when Sarah tried to bring it up with Milton, he gently silenced her. He felt genuine love for the baby, he told her, therefore she was his. Sarah and Milton made the most of their time together, for it was clear that they were well matched. Yet they both recognized that the pleasure of each other's company was a privilege, a gift that could be reclaimed whenever the giver had a yearning. Sarah had sworn that her knowledge of that brutal fact would not be the death of her.

As the wagon bumped and rolled, she reviewed every word she knew, searching in vain for one noun or adjective expansive enough to describe how the day's events had taught her to see herself: exhausted, alone, and all out of surprises.

Having helped himself to Silent Mary's baked goods (without offering Sarah so much as a nibble), Holtzclaw deduced that he had been perhaps too hasty in his consumption. Midpoint between Placid Hall and Two Forks, his stomach had grown angry and demanded relief. He halted the wagon at the side of a tree-lined road, climbed down, and hurried into a thicket of vines. Sarah could see the top of his head as he squatted and grunted. She could also see a rock, substantial yet handy, on the ground between him and the wagon. She studied it, imagining what she could do with it and calculating the speed and stealth she'd need to cover the distance. Slowly, quietly, she swung her legs over the side of the wagon. Before she could lower her feet to the ground, a flicker of motion in the trees above her head made her pause. She looked up and saw, crouching on a branch, a creature from another world.

It rested on one haunch, the other leg fully extended along the length of the branch, with both arms stretched upward and grasping an overhead limb. The being's clothes were made to resemble bark, enabling it to blend almost seamlessly against its background. Most striking was its face, in broad strokes of brown and green painted so closely together that no flesh showed. Was it a haint? An angel? Sarah was too awestruck to hazard a guess. Without losing balance, the creature folded an elegant arm and placed a finger to its lips. Sarah nearly gasped when the creature leaped and landed gracefully on silent feet. It squatted and, securing Sarah's attention, drew in the dirt with its index finger. After making sure Sarah saw the marks it made, it rubbed them away. Quick as death, it scampered up a tree and returned to its perch.

His bowels settled, Holtzclaw came back to the wagon and noticed a glow on Sarah's face. He chuckled to himself, concluding that her radiance was a sign of the excitement he assumed he aroused in Stolen wenches.

Sarah lived to experience even more surprises, but none as wondrous as her encounter with the mystical figure that swooped down from the trees. She knew then that she would always remember the angel's marks in the dirt, even if she never learned to make sense of them. The cryptic letters burned in her memory as if they had been written in flames.

"In Due Time," the words read.

VI
Gleam

Ransom

White was the color of grief, but fabric of that hue was exceedingly rare among Stolen. Day to day, most wore rags or converted sacks. Even those who toiled indoors and thus required finer garments found their clothes easily tarnished amid the dirt, sweat, and dust of daily labor. So it was my task to keep the scraps of mourning cloth clean. I washed them myself, stirring them in a pot of boiling lye and laying them out to bleach in the sun. I kept them tucked safely away until such occasions as Milton's homegoing. Then I would hand them out for the gathered to gird themselves. Some tied the strips around waists, others around arms, and still others around their heads.

Burials were held in the day, as soon after death as possible. Milton's was delayed until Greene shared his thoughts in a speech I'm told was unusually brief. Afterward stones, leaves, pieces of bark, a bracelet made of cornsilk and twine, the special bandages that eased Milton's last moments, and his clay mug were all placed in a bag and lowered into the grave with his body. Once the grave was filled in, a bowl was placed upside down atop the mound. On its bottom was an X, representing a crossroads, inscribed inside a circle. Monuments of this kind, many reduced to fragments and picked apart by birds and other creatures, adorned every grave in Hush Harbor.

Homegoings were nighttime affairs that depended on the goodwill of Thieves. With their permission, Stolen from various farms could meet and support one another in a ritual that started off somber but typically ended on a note of triumph. Often one needn't know the newly dead to participate; our observances offered an occasion to convene with kindred spirits and refresh our temperaments by forming new bonds. Nearly thirty were on hand to send Milton off. Looking about the clearing, I was disheartened that Sarah was not among them, although I could easily imagine the reason for her absence. William's attendance was a welcome surprise, for he had made a practice of forgoing such gatherings. I attributed his presence to Margaret's influence, as she busied herself with tying his cloth around his arm.

Torches placed along the perimeter of the clearing pushed the shadows back into the surrounding trees. After allowing a pair of fiddlers to enter the rough circle we'd formed, we joined hands. The musicians touched off the event with subtle bowing. A wistful tune floated up from the fiddles, a soft wave of sound that enveloped us like a caress. We waited, taking it all in, each of us using the moment to remember Milton, some kind word or gesture that warmed our hearts. When the fiddling slowed and the melody faded to a faint refrain, I stepped forward.

"Sistren, brethren," I said. "Shall we hum?"

We pursed our lips and released the common sound first forged in the bellies of ships to overcome our mismatched tongues, tongues that came from dozens of villages in Africa. Silent Mary's hum was most powerful of all, a lively purr providing a richness of expression her silence routinely denied. It felt at such times that we could move the earth with our vibrations: bottomless, resonant, and so much older than ourselves. Then we shifted to a lower frequency, and a handful of Milton's celebrants took turns testifying against a backdrop of handclaps and rattling bones.

Two women spoke fondly of Milton's dancing. *Hum, hum, clap.*

Cato praised his timely wit. *Hum, hum, clap.*

"With his drawings, he showed me Canada," Zander said. "Africa too." *Hum, hum, clap.*

A space opened between hum and clap, and Margaret urged William to walk through it. Hesitantly, he entered the ring.

"Some of us believe Milton's on his way back to Africa," he began, "where he will find rest in the loving arms of his Ancestors. Others think he has returned to the clay from which his Creator formed him."

William turned to Margaret for reassurance. She smiled at him and nodded.

"For all of us," he continued, "one truth is certain: he will no longer have to struggle alongside us, here in the hell that Thieves made." William paused, as if he had more to say. Apparently he thought better of it, for he shook his head and left the circle. Margaret took his hand, and Cato clapped him on the shoulder.

I took the ensuing lull as my cue to resume. Raising my voice, I encouraged us to move from mourning to movement, from grief to joy. Every time I swayed the crowd, a voice would ring out in response, confirming my point.

"Milton is not lost," I said.

"No!"

"Milton is not finished."

"That's right!"

"Milton is not departed."

"I see him still!"

"Milton is not broken or bent or bowed."

"Preach!"

"What he is . . . is free."

"Well!"

"Free, sistren and brethren! Free from all *this*. For Milton, every morning from now on will be a great getting up!"

The entire circle took up the chant: "Free! Free! Free!" We repeated it until we reached a fever pitch, our voices strained with excitement. Unwinding the white strips from our bodies, we let our sadness float to the ground. Women kicked their heels above their heads. Men twisted and flexed. In a whirl of laughter, wild notes, and hallelujahs, we shook and cried. Cried and shook. The fiddlers took up their instruments again and committed to furious bowing, sawing at the strings in a frenzy. The bone-clappers rattled a staccato accompaniment. Little Zander, bellowing and sprinting, flipped end over end, backward and forward, forward and back. We could have celebrated Milton's freedom until dawn if not for the swift rush of time. Sunrise was not far away. The fields would not wait.

At my signal, we slowed our movements, allowing our rhapsody to cool to manageable warmth. After affectionate goodbyes and the clasping of hands, Milton's mourners departed with haste. Though they had obtained passes for this night, many had a ways to go. No longer muted by fiddling and humming and jubilant shouts, the regular sounds of night reemerged to claim the clearing. Margaret lingered, helping me to gather the white strips that had been strewn about in our delirium. As she placed the last remnant in my pouch, she turned to me. William stood close by, waiting for her.

"Preacher," she said, "what if God is a Thief?"

I had the feeling she was asking for William as much as for herself.

"I want God to be bigger than Thieves," I told her. "I want God to be bigger than *all* of this."

"And is he?"

"I don't know."

Margaret looked into my eyes, first one and then the other, as if her staring might give greater clarity to my words.

"Yet you believe," she said.

"Yes."

"What good is in that?"

"Maybe none. But there's no harm in it either."

"You got a strange faith, Preacher."

"It's a strange world, is it not?"

She considered this. A half smile formed on her lips, suggesting she was satisfied. "Indeed it is," she said.

She moved away, but William appeared in front of me before she had completely turned her back. He regarded me with his usual intensity, not cruelly but with no special kindness either.

"You're supposed to have all the answers," he said. It felt like an accusation.

I chuckled and strapped my pouch across my shoulder. "I wish it were only that," I told him. "I don't even have all the questions."

Margaret

When I had seven harvests behind me, I got this habit of staring down the road, waiting for my mother to come back from wherever she was sold. Standing in the yard, I came to know every clod and pebble of the lane leading away from the farm. I could mark the point at which the heat turned to ribbons that waved above the ground, the way the grass grew on both sides of the path, and the movement of shadows as the hours passed. I imagined my mother's voice in every gust of wind stirring the landmark oak that leaned above the turnoff to my Thief's lands, could hear her whispering through branches arching over every horse and wagon that traveled underneath. As months turned into years, I kept on hoping that the swirls of dust kicked up by hooves would magically uncoil to reveal my mother, walking toward me with arms outstretched and a smile on her face. No commotion behind me, not even the threat of danger, could sway me from my post. More than once a kindly Stolen adult swooped me up and carried me away from likely punishment as I kicked and screamed in protest. It took me four harvests to get over this tendency, and to this day I can see things at a distance better than things that are near me.

Goldwood was the only farm I had known before coming to

Two Forks, having arrived there while still in my mother's belly. It belonged to Elbridge Hooper, who received much of his wealth through his marriage to a pleasant widow named Abigail. She entertained few guests other than her brother, Jeremiah, whom she loved fiercely. As for Elbridge, he favored being on horseback to standing on the ground. He was fond of sitting tall in the saddle and watching over his captives as they labored, but he never dirtied his own hands. His brother-in-law was helpful in this regard. Jeremiah was a nuisance, but his bent for farming made it easier for Elbridge to put up with him. What we knew of the Hooper family came from the Stolen laboring in the main house. From them we learned that Elbridge spared most of his kindness for his beloved daughter, an only child with about twenty harvests behind her. With the young lady recently married and moved away, he spent his days taking long solitary trips beyond his estate into neighboring territories. He had just returned from such an outing when the trouble began, troubles that Elbridge could have avoided, it was said, if he had simply bothered to get off his horse every once in a while.

The yard was full of active Stolen. I was working on the trash gang, pulling weeds, when the door to the main house flew open. Jeremiah rushed across the threshold, dashing down the veranda steps with Elbridge running after him. He'd managed only a few strides before Elbridge brought him down.

"Take your hands off me!" Jeremiah yelled.

"Not until you're dead!" Elbridge yelled back.

Even with just seven harvests behind me I had seen men go at it like hounds. But in every instance they had been Stolen, sometimes fighting because their Thieves forced them to. In other cases, the fight had started because of a quarrel over a woman or something as simple as an ear of corn. Never, however, had I seen two Thieves dressed in fine clothes tussling in the dirt. The mistress of the house, fluttering like a hen, wailed from the veranda. Neither Elbridge nor Jeremiah was much of a fighter, and neither was in the springtime of life. Mostly they just tore each other's collars and mussed each other's hair. Four or five Stolen men, all of them better with their fists, watched them from a distance. The mistress hollered for them to do something, but they knew better. They found new tasks until the Thieves wore themselves out, stumbled to their feet, and staggered inside.

The details quickly reached the quarters. Elbridge had discovered what some Stolen had already known: his wife had been having relations with her own brother and had been doing so for more than twenty years. At dusk, I played with the other children, taking turns at jumping rope and making up stories for our topsy-turvy dolls. All the while, we listened to the chatter of the adults who watched over us from their cabin stoops. They said things like "right under his nose!" and "all their lives!" The laughter died down as the sky grew dark, and the jokes gave way to more personal concerns. What, if anything, would happen to Goldwood? What would happen to us?

If my mother was uneasy, she didn't share her worries with me. After feeding and washing me, she sang my favorite lullaby until I fell asleep.

Hush-a-by and don't you cry,
And go to sleep, little baby;
When you wake you shall have some cake
And ride a pretty little horsey.

You shall have a little canoe
And a little bit of a paddle;
You shall have a little red mule
And a little bitty saddle.

The black and the bay, the sorrel and the gray,
All belong to my baby.

Gleam

So hush-a-by and don't you cry
And go to sleep, little baby.

It was the last night I spent in her arms. Her face has faded from my memory, but her voice lingers.

In the main house, a quick bargain had been struck by lamplight. As Elbridge glared sternly from the porch and Abigail wept somewhere within, Jeremiah left early in the morning, escorted by a pair of hired men and taking with him a company of Stolen that included my mother. Our parting was fierce and terrible, a desperate embrace before my mother was coffled and tethered behind a wagon. The air rushed from my body as I strained against the arms that conspired to hold me back. While my sobs and urgent prayers joined the others erupting all around me, Jeremiah's procession continued down the road that would hold my gaze for years to come.

I did more staring than crying as I grew, not having much time to feel sorry for myself. Nor, of course, did I have the maternal breast on which I had once pressed such sadness. What good was weeping with no mother to rock me gently and offer tender words?

I continued to toil at Goldwood for another seven harvests until Elbridge was found dead, slumped over in his saddle. His will bequeathed Two Forks, another of his estates, to his daughter, the skittish young lady whose bloodline had by then become an open question. I was sent there along with several others to serve her and her husband, a man named Cannonball Greene. When I arrived, they had been married for nearly ten years and together controlled three farms and ten thousand acres. I soon learned that in the quarters Mrs. Greene was known, with no hint of affection, as Screech Owl.

She rarely appeared during my first years at Two Forks, and I seldom had reason to venture near the main house when she did. When I came to make my home with William at Placid Hall, I saw her most often during her regular trips to the family grave-yard, where three small plots held the remains of her fallen children. Screech Owl's frailty and hardship in childbirth had resulted in infants who never lived to see their first harvest. It was only when glimpsing her private mourning that I ever felt something like tenderness toward her, for I had a notion of the burden she shouldered.

Long before William came into my life, I had learned to grasp both sides of my situation, to consider that perhaps somewhere my mother had been looking down a similar lane, a dusty, winding path that would lead to me. There was such loss, such emptiness in that possibility that no part of being a Stolen mother or daughter seemed to offer any reward; either way, one wound up losing. As for being a daughter, I had had no choice in the matter. But as I grew up and womanhood came despite my every effort to delay it, I resolved, as did many Stolen women, that I would never give birth, never be yanked from the arms of a child and dragged down a road that she would fix her eyes on for years after. To our dismay, we soon learned that we had no say over our bodies and what could or could not be done with them. If bringing forth new life meant I could stay with William I was willing, even eager, to do it.

I hadn't known that Stolen men worried in the same way that women did until I met William. In most men, the craving for women's flesh outweighed every other concern. But while William's appetite was strong, he managed to keep it under control. His restraint, at first a marvel to me, began to unsettle me enough to keep me awake nights. Although he often argued otherwise, I didn't need him to remind me that few Stolen ever had a chance to finish life with the mate they started out with, let alone with one they had chosen, that the odds were against us regardless of Cannonball Greene's unsteady whims. It was true, I knew, that even fewer of us got to see our children grow up. Milton's dying before getting to know his daughter, Silent Mary's lifelong silence after losing her child, William's own obsession with the dead children he had encountered long ago—all of these things only made him more wary. At the same time, he was troubled to know that Greene saw our slowness at making a baby as a failure that needed solving. Distracted, he agreed to accompany me to the homegoing without quite realizing what he'd consented to.

He didn't know I had acquired a distraction of my own. After watching Sarah leave with Holtzclaw, Ben sent Clarence away and presumed to walk beside me back to the quarter. I tried to stop him in his tracks by assuring him I had no interest in his company.

"No matter," he told me, leaning in close. I feared for a moment that he was preparing to swipe my face with his disgusting tongue. "Boss Greene told me I'm next in line if you and Billy Boy keep coming up empty."

A fierce pain seized my chest, making it hard to breathe. "What do you mean?" I asked him.

"You know," he said. He grabbed himself. "You know what 'next in line' means, I'm sure. One shot is all I need, although you'll be wanting more than that. I've got more sap than a sweetgum."

I moved to slap him but he caught my wrist.

"Careful now," he warned.

"William will kill you," I said.

"And Boss Greene will skin him directly," he said with a grin. "Or else sell him away. Where will that leave you?"

"Not with you," I said, tearing myself from his grip. "Never with you."

Ben chuckled. "You go on ahead, mind yourself. Big Ben's more patient than you think."

He left no telltale bruise upon my flesh, but his nasty words got under my skin and lodged there like a hornet's barb. Still, I managed to nearly forget them during Milton's homegoing. With William beside me, I lost myself in the singing and shouting. The brief audience with Preacher afterward also made me feel better, but only for a while. By the time we returned to our cabin a nagging nervousness began to grow in me, rising and swelling until it became a desperate yearning.

In the wee hours, I took William into my arms, determined to make him finish what he started. I rubbed his back while he moved inside me. "I'm standing over yonder," I whispered.

"I'm on free soil. Nothing between you and me but open ground. No whips, no Thieves, no hounds out for our hides. Just grass and sunlight and warm gentle breezes. Run to me," I urged him. "Take my hand. Run until you can't run anymore."

He took my hand and together we moved in great strides, until he crossed over.

William

I was glad I had gone to Milton's homegoing, although I didn't intend to admit as much to Margaret. Singing and dancing will never be among my favorite pastimes. Yet I was drawn to the raw feeling that seemed to flow among all the participants; the event produced in me a powerful happiness I had seldom felt. I still had my doubts about Ransom. I had long thought him self-important and full of secrets, and possibly even a spy for Greene. However, during a brief moment to myself in our cabin the next day, I recalled the good words he had spoken. He had said nothing that struck me as odd or deceitful. Besides, I had no disagreement at all with his insistence that Milton was indeed free. I was also pleasantly surprised that he readily confessed to not knowing everything, or even knowing whether what he believed was true. I noted his kindness toward Margaret, which seemed to come from honest affection and nothing more. I got a notion that perhaps we had more in common than I was prepared to admit. I had long been accused of believing in nothing, but my days—and nights—with Margaret so awakened my spirit that I feared it would weaken me and lead to my undoing. While I placed no stock in the muttering of sevens or begging a god who lived in the sky, I had nonetheless come upon a tremendous faith. I believed in her. I believed in us.

I found myself taking Mama and Papa Root from my pouch, feeling the weight of the wood in my hands. They were meant to be seen as the beginning of a very old story, Guinea Jack had told me. How did Margaret and I fit into it? How would it end?

"Aren't you too old to be playing with dolls?"

Little Zander, ever light on his feet, had appeared in my doorway without making a sound. I quickly put Mama and Papa Root out of sight.

"You know better than to sneak up on a body," I said.

"When I land," Zander said, "I make even less noise. Did you hear that whip-poor-will last night?"

Margaret had kept me so involved during the night that I heard little beside the sounds of our loving, which we struggled to stifle. I decided to play along.

"Maybe," I told him. "Why?"

"Well, that wasn't a whip-poor-will." Leaning against the doorframe, Zander balanced on one leg, his heel resting on his opposite knee.

"Then what was it?"

"Not a what but a who."

"Zander, I have no appetite for riddles. Who was it?"

"Preacher."

"Ransom? Explain."

"He knows more about angels than he lets on. I know this about him. I saw you and Margaret talking to him after the homegoing. I followed him when he went off on his own. Tracked him to the creek. He made the bird sound, and a Buba Yali answered back. Dropped down from the trees. It wasn't my first time following Preacher. I'd seen the two of them before. They talked. The Buba Yali took off."

"And?"

"And that's all. I ran back to my cabin before Preacher could spot me. I knew better than to talk to him about it. He would just put me off."

"How do you mean?"

"As I said, I know about him. I had seen those two before."

By then I had figured that Zander was caught up in another of his fanciful spells. I wondered if this one, like his dream about two angels wrestling a demon, was at least partly true. "Tell me what happened," I said, "but try using words that folks without wings would understand."

"You're funny, William. I'd wager not many people know that, seeing how much you contemplate most everything. The first time I saw them, the angel dipped Preacher into the water. Baptized him. What I can't figure, though, is why he needed it. He's been saved a long time. God's got him in the palm of his hand."

"How come you always talk of such things?"

He smiled. "How come you don't?"

In truth, I was beginning to think about such things more than I spoke about them aloud. I decided to save my answer for another day. "Did you confront him about what you'd seen?"

"I asked him some questions."

"What did he say?"

" 'In due time,' " he told me. " 'In due time.' "

I stored away Zander's odd chatter to turn over in my mind at a favorable time. As summer went on, I sometimes returned to it, sifting the words in search of hidden meaning, but each time I came up with nothing.

Greene had thus far chosen to keep us working in the pit without the help of an additional man. He was busy, Pandora reported, preparing his "studies" after attracting interest from a local academy. Some days it seemed that Ransom was present more often than the Thief of Placid Hall. He became a valued adviser to Margaret, talking with her often about life, death, and fate. Clearly she had decided I was unfit for such lofty talk. When I asked her why she seldom mentioned such matters to me, she dismissed me as a nonbeliever. With a halting tongue, I assured her that there were more kinds of belief than she supposed. One thing was certain: I lacked Preacher's skill at speaking in a way that brought people over to his way of thinking. My childish jealousy was cooled by the presence of others during his sessions with Margaret; his most interested followers had come to make up a group I knew well. Besides her, Little Zander, Pandora, and Cato were in attendance, along with Silent Mary when she could get a rare break from her duties. I pressed Cato for details after the questions I put to Margaret shed no new light. But he'd only offer some excuse before heading off to an errand he claimed couldn't wait.

Cato

I had begun to consider the notion that Isaac's spectral visit had served a critical purpose that would reveal itself in a timely fashion. I had searched Hush Harbor in vain for signs of his presence while William and I turned over soil for Milton's final resting place. When he finally showed up a few weeks later, I nearly asked him what had delayed him. He came up behind me while I was stealing a chance to wash my face in the stream. I squatted at the edge, cupping the water in my hands. After my years of anguish, I had finally grown comfortable with looking at my own reflection. For the first time in many harvests, I had a fondness for what I saw.

"Killed the snake, didn't you?"

I turned to him, smiling. He was dressed in finery that I couldn't recognize, like a prosperous gentleman from a foreign land. Nothing about his costume suggested he had ever known bondage or hunger. His boots gleamed brightly, as did the buttons on his jacket. It seemed too bulky and hot for our climate, but his brow was dry and he showed no signs of discomfort.

"Isaac," I said. "I've never told anyone about that."

I had begun to despise serpents with a powerful fervor when Iris died. They reminded me of the fear that paralyzed me when I should have stepped forward to defend her. If I had intervened, if I had run after the cart, risked everything to try to convince Greene not to sell her, I might have altered the string of consequences, traded my life for hers. But I hesitated when her new Thief ordered me to remain still, and in my mind that awful timidity set a snake loose to wander in front of the cart carrying Iris, frighten the horse, and set our tragedy in motion. There was no such snake, of course, but it became my private torment. I dreamed about it often for years after losing Iris. Time passed, and as my affection for Pandora grew, the snake faded from my consciousness. But then one night it came back. In the dream, I was placing the last layer of soil on Milton's grave when I turned and saw it, nearly as high as my shoulders, rearing up and hissing. I killed it with the spade in my hands, separating its head from its body.

Isaac smiled. "But it's dead, right?"

I stood up and looked around. No one else was in sight.

As he had done before, Isaac seemed to read my thoughts. "I'm here just for you, my friend," he said. "No one else can see me. Just carry on as you were."

I took his suggestion and ambled toward the quarters.

"There's nothing between you and Pandora now," he continued. "Nothing to hold you back."

"I am powerfully partial to her."

"Then what are you waiting for?"

"I'm afraid of failing her," I confessed, "the way I did Iris."

"You won't," Isaac said. "And Iris? She understands. Do you know why you survived the pain Greene put you through after you stepped up to save Nila? Do you know why you're still breathing?"

"The only thing I know for certain is that I couldn't have lived through it without you."

Isaac chuckled softly. "You would have survived anyway. Because you're not meant to die here. Neither is Pandora. I reckon Ransom has told you as much."

It was true. In the weeks since Milton's death, the preacher had

been filling our heads with bold ideas that he claimed were proph-
ecies. They were so daring and wonderful and reckless that I was
inclined to dismiss them as mere nonsense, no more credible than
the stories in the Book of Thieves. Yet they infected me, seizing my
imagination at the most inopportune moments.

"It's time you told her your feelings, Cato."

He turned to go. I bade him goodbye, then called to him before he got too far. I asked him how he found out about the snake
and how he could speak for Iris.

He smiled. "I'm an Ancestor, remember? We know everything."

Up to this point, my "courtship" of Pandora had consisted mostly
of long glances and small courtesies that she had returned in kind.
My reticence and Pandora's patience had prompted much mirth
on the part of Ben and Clarence. Ben would scratch, spit, and
offer horrid suggestions while Clarence cheered his every word.
Although I was occasionally tempted to silence Ben with a blow
to the skull, their goading had no lasting effect. It was the visit
from Isaac that stirred me to further action. With the snake banished from my dreams and Isaac's encouragement in my thoughts,
I sought her out on Sunday, when Cannonball Greene granted us
a brief respite following our services with Ransom. Silent Mary offered Pandora and me some light victuals that we toted in a basket
to a remote spot. We had our meal on a blanket, eating in comfortable silence until at last I was moved to speak. Pandora reclined on
her back while I sat beside her.

"I am tenderly disposed toward you," I said.

She smiled. "Anybody can see that, Cato. I'm most apprecia-
tive of your kindness."

"It's a powerful feeling, Pandora. It's in here," I said, laying my
hand on my heart, "but I don't know how to get it out."

"Leave it there," Pandora told me. "Let me get it."

She reached for me, pressed her lips softly to mine.

"I haven't been with a woman since Iris," I said. "I mean, really been with a woman. I don't, I can't—"

"Shush, man."

I lay above her, supporting my weight. I felt her hands moving on me. We kissed again, longer.

"See," she said. "Seems to me you're doing just fine."

The next morning, I felt William's eyes on me when we gathered at the water trough. When Cupid was foreman, we counted ourselves fortunate to briefly wet our throats before commencing with our labors. In contrast, William was generous with the water, and morning gatherings had become an opportunity for fellowship and fortitude. As our crew made its way to the pit, William asked me to accompany him to the tool shed. He had appeared to be taking the measure of me, pondering some nagging riddle. I had begun the day determined to speak privately with William and was pleased to find him similarly moved. Since we had last spoken, I had had time to fully appreciate Pandora's commitment to me, as well as the significance of Isaac's words. I dared to believe that his prophecy, as it were, applied to William as well. He wasn't meant to die at Placid Hall.

We arrived at the shed and he pretended to look for a pickax.

"I have questions," he began.

"As do I," I said, cutting him off.

He squinted at me. "All right, then. Shall I?"

"I'll speak first. William, what do you mean when you say we are brothers?"

"I mean a life is no little thing, and I owe mine to you. I believe I have been clear."

"Brothers share confidences, yes?"

"Yes."

"I have a notion. One that should be guarded with care."

"You have my word it goes no further."

I stood directly in front of him, placing my hands on his shoulders. "What would you do if a Thief offered to tell you a story?"

"You know," he replied. "I would—Wait. Are you suggesting that we—"

"Run," I said. "Let's run." I was certain William had thought of such things, had imagined somehow being somewhere else. He often declined to indulge in our speculation about freedom, whether it was possible and how it would feel. He dismissed it as useless chatter, but we all could see that he was just as vulnerable to such visions. Who among us hadn't at some point found himself stuck in reverie, looking at nothing and dreaming of everything?

"The things we've been through," I continued. "The things we've done. They are all pointing to this one result."

William held my gaze, searching my eyes for some sign that I was anything but deadly serious. He turned away and again busied himself with the tools. "Just us?"

"No," I replied. "Pandora and Margaret. Zander."

"He's just a boy."

"A boy who can steer by the stars. Can you do that?"

William hoisted a pickax on his shoulder. "The five of us alone," he said softly.

"Not entirely," I said. "We will have help."

William

At Cato's urging, I agreed to speak with Ransom. But he disappeared until the last days of summer. His followers explained that he was on a tour of distant plantations where there was urgent need of the Holy Word. As always, his ability to move so freely about the world of Thieves made me uneasy. I understood that he could talk his way out of trouble—if anyone could do that, it would be Ransom—but so often? He seemed to travel according to his own schedule, unrestrained by Thieves. But I knew that couldn't be. Nor had I forgotten my curious talk with Little Zander. I continued to suspect that either he hadn't told me everything he'd seen or that he had confided in me as some kind of test, to determine whether I was able to view the preacher as an ally and not a foe. It was Zander's words I was thinking of when I finally met up with Ransom on a Sunday in September. In the long, sparse patch of earth between the flanking rows of cabins, Stolen were relaxing and amusing themselves in the few hours left before dark. Margaret and Zander had joined Cato and Pandora on a blanket under a shade tree, laughing and talking quietly. To keep their courtship hidden, Cato and Pandora seldom appeared together. Greene

Gleam

had shown no signs of pairing Pandora with anyone, wanting her, perhaps, for himself.

Ransom and I sat several yards away on a crude bench made of castoff planks. He tore off a piece of the bread Silent Mary had made him and offered it to me, but I declined.

"Look at Cato," he said, smiling. "I do believe he has acquired the gleam."

It was true that Cato was looking better, even younger. I had always guessed that he had seen perhaps ten harvests before I came into this world. A few months ago I had begun to think of him as maybe five harvests older. Watching him trade sly smiles with Pandora, I was beginning to think we were the same age.

"Gleam of what?" I asked.

"Illumination."

"What does that mean?"

"I mean to say that he sees clearly now. Clearer than he ever has."

Ransom went on to tell me about a group of "agents," he called them, who secretly helped Stolen escape to freedom. He said the group was called the Chariot and that all of its members had sworn to battle Thievery until death. Cato had seen the light, he told me.

"That's why he looks so different. He has his eyes on freedom. When he leaves—when you all leave—you'll have the Chariot to guide and assist you."

"The Chariot," I repeated. "Who knows about this?"

He nodded toward my friends. "Everyone under that tree."

I had heard of the Chariot, of course. Up to then I'd figured it was another of those strange notions handed down from mother to child, like the importance of saying your seven before going to bed. I stood up suddenly.

"Why should I trust you?"

Ransom looked pained. He sighed. "Sit down, please. Please."

I resumed my seat.

"You're strong, William. Brave too, sometimes to the point of foolishness. But you're not so smart, are you, son?"

"I'm not your son. It sounds as if you all have it all planned. What do they need me for?"

"Your courage. Cupid beat every Stolen man on this plantation. But he never even raised his voice at you, to say nothing of a fist. Because he sensed your lack of fear. It's a rare quality, you see. When you go north, you can't possibly anticipate everything you might run into. When runaways encounter an unwelcome surprise, it's helpful to have on hand someone who doesn't falter."

I considered this for a moment. "Cato says we aren't meant to die here," I said. "He thinks our future is somewhere yonder."

Ransom smiled. "You should listen to him. As I've said, he's seen the light."

He offered me bread again. I accepted it.

"Another consideration, William. Cannonball wants to keep you in the *right now*. He wants you to study the possibility that you can find comfort in it, a certain stillness that shields you from the wickedness sticking to everything. The last thing he wants you to think about is the what's to come—or worse, about what could be. When Stolen start thinking about days ahead, that is when Greene's world ends."

To succeed with such a scheme, we would need time, lots of it, to build up our strength and collect information. That, at least, is what I thought. In our cabin that night, Margaret quickly corrected me.

"We can't just up and go. We have to plan," I said.

Margaret had difficulty remaining in one place when she was anxious or upset. She paced our small room with such vigor that

I expected the dirt floor to crumble beneath her bare heels. "We *have* been planning, William. You could have joined us, but you've always avoided Ransom like he's the enemy. You're far more kind to Greene than you are to him."

"I assure you I am not. I simply see Greene for what he is. I look at Ransom—I used to look at Ransom—and I couldn't tell. I understand now." In truth I still wasn't entirely convinced that the preacher wouldn't betray us after we'd set out on our way, but I kept my doubts to myself.

Margaret glared at me. "Well, you were slow in the understanding. We like Ransom because he reminds us there's something else yonder, not just these awful places where we bleed and sweat to fatten Thieves' purses. He helps us remember that. But not you. You don't want to hear about it, much less talk about it."

"That's so I can go on. That's so I can get through the day. That's so—"

Margaret turned her face from me and offered the palm of her hand in its place. "Enough with the soft talk. I'm feeling hard right now. I need you to be the same way. I will be heading north before it gets too cold to go. Winter's not far off. I want you with me."

"You can't just waltz out of here as merry as you please. And if you could, what would you do next?"

"Waltz? Do I look like a woman who waltzes? Do I love like a woman who waltzes? Remember who you're talking to, William. Remember who I am."

"You're many women in one. And I want all of them to live." I was quite satisfied with what I said, but Margaret would have none of it.

"The longer we live *here*, the more we lose. Fingers. Teeth. Tongues. People we love. I'm sick of losing, William."

I raised my hands and backed away in surrender. "Hear me, Margaret. I'm committed to this. I'm committed to you."

"Then you'd best get moving. Looks to me like you're standing still."

"You've endured this hell for harvest after harvest. And suddenly you want to leave right now. Why? What's changed?"

Her eyes glistening with tears, she took my hands and placed them gently on her belly. "I got your child in me," she said.

I remembered the night I let her be stronger than me, when I let her pull me into her and keep me there until I was spent. The night she told me to run and run and run.

VII

Band
of
Angels

The man might as well have been underwater. Cannonball Greene could hear him speaking, could see his lips moving, but the sound that emerged was nearly indecipherable. Greene's sense of wrong, his creeping dread, and the awful gnawing in his stomach so absorbed him that simple conversation proved elusive. That morning, Silent Mary had offered sustenance with her usual kitchen wizardry, but he had left his breakfast untouched. His abstinence was no reflection of her skills; the simple truth was no food on earth could distract him from his present woes. Six months ago, Cupid, to whom he had given so much, had taken off and left no trace. He had yet to fully recover from that loss when he woke up one crisp fall day—after a weekend of stomach troubles and wretched squatting over chamber pots—and learned that five more of his possessions had vanished in the night. What was the point of caring for and feeding niggas if they could so easily fall prey to depravity and engage in such reckless, unhelpful conduct? After he'd gotten to the bottom of this mystery, when he'd recovered his ungrateful property and punished them for their transgressions, he'd turn his discoveries into another chapter on the management of nigga infirmities. Others had already come up with good names for certain kinds of nigga hysterics—solid, authoritative words like *drapetomania* and *rascality*. He could do better than those, he was certain, once his stomach had regained its customary calmness and the infernal throbbing in his temples had subsided. In the meantime, he was stuck on his veranda, forced to endure the company of this miscreant who promised to bring them back alive. Or had he only promised to bring them back?

"If anyone knows niggas, it's me," the man seemed to be saying. "Consequently I know a nigga conspiracy when I smell one. This scheme reeks so mightily that soon it will disturb the nostrils of our Lord in heaven."

Greene stared at Josiah Norbrook. If the man knew anything at all, it was failure. His gambling and whoring were notorious, and he had frittered away his feeble fortune with such avid stupidity that now he was forced to accept work utterly unfit for men of stature. Not that he'd ever had much of that. Greene struggled to remind himself why he'd enlisted Norbrook's services in the first place. Because he had a reputation for skillful hunting and hurting. Because he didn't have a kind bone in his body. Because he could proceed with the cold cruelty the task demanded.

Realizing that Norbrook was leaning forward expectantly, Greene began to suspect a gap in the conversation that custom determined he should fill. How long had the silence lingered? How far had his mind wandered? He sat upright with a start.

"Pardon me, Mr. Norbrook," he said. "I've been out of sorts."

His guest nodded in sympathy. "They'll do that to you."

"It's the bucks," Greene said. "The wenches are no bother. They don't think much, and they do what they're told. I could give one my firearm to hold and then lie down for a long nap. I'd wake with her watching over me, cradling the weapon gently in her arms and cooing to it as if it were a suckling babe."

Norbrook grunted. "I don't trust wenches of any color."

"Wenches are only one color, Mr. Norbrook. Our women are ladies. Regarding the bucks, only one of them seems capable of this kind of betrayal, and that would be William. I have prized him, perhaps against my better judgment. He has a quality of manhood exceedingly rare among his kind. He will parley with you and seem to be suitably obedient. Then he leaves and you'll say, 'Was that nigga looking me in the eye the whole time?' Cato has no such worrisome habit. He either looks off in the distance or, more submissively, down at the ground. He's not capable of harming a fly. When he helped Cupid run, I kept Cato chained on account of principle and as a lesson for the others. But he curled up next to that post for as long as I told him to, whether he was in irons or not."

Norbrook swallowed the last of his tea and wiped his mouth with his sleeve. Then he belched. "If you ask me," he said, "that's the kind to never turn your back on. When he's looking off like you say, he's thinking about running. When he's looking at the ground, he's counting the paces between his dirty hands and your pink throat."

Greene glared at his guest. "I did not ask you, in point of fact. Spare me your peculiar . . . philosophy."

Norbrook considered Greene. If a fellow spoke to him so dismissively in a less formal setting, say a tavern, he'd bounce a mug off his crown and pocket his coins in the bargain. Greene was talking to him as if he hadn't sold William to him in the first place. While he'd trapped and skinned many a buck since then, something about that particular nigga still stuck in his craw.

Norbrook kept his hands to himself and said, smiling, "That's right, I forget you're a keen observer of the inferior species. Mind you, an inferior scalp or two could get lost in this business."

"No scalps, Norbrook. I want them alive and whole."

"Alive it is, then, as long as you realize that property recovery is a dangerous venture. Accidents happen. Niggas tend to lose parts. Ears. Toes. Things of that nature."

Greene stood suddenly. "Enough of this dithering, sir. I believe you are sufficiently fortified. Now go to it. Please leave my property at once."

Norbrook shrugged and then slowly rose. "Like I told you, no need for unseemly worry. None of these niggas know north from south. Chance is good they're shuffling in a circle, bumping their woolly heads on low-hanging branches. Once a nigga had a week's advantage and I still caught him before he reached the county line. Dumb as fence posts, they are. Caught him holed up in a hollow log, smelling worse than a skunk, big yellow teeth just a-chattering. Trust me, when I catch your niggas they will be glad I did. No such thing as a nigga who can fend for himself."

Greene said nothing, silently conceding that Norbrook spoke the truth. A nigga took off from time to time but usually came back, either dragged in chains or stumbling half-crazed with his tail between his legs.

"Suit yourself though," Norbrook said. "I'll commence."

Norbrook was muttering to himself as he approached Greene's stables, pondering, as he often did, the great cosmic injustice that forced him to toil like a common man while all about him lesser beings relaxed in palatial splendor. What a torment it had been to sit and sip tea with Greene, whose hands were as soft as a woman's! He was nothing like the rugged charmer Norbrook saw when he stood in front of his looking glass. The mirror reflected a self-made man, although on some liquored-up mornings he could recognize neither the self nor the man. Only the prospect of hunting and trapping kept him from sliding into a daylong, alcohol-fueled wallow in fetid self-pity. Ever since he'd taken up the trade, he'd never run into a nigga clever enough to hide his tracks for more than a day or two. His mind fixed on the memory of his favorite captures, he entered the stable and roused his horse.

Except the horse would not be moved. It wasn't asleep, but

it declined to respond to his commands. Slapping at it with his crop was equally fruitless. It shrunk away each time he tried to mount it.

"Yip! Let's go! What's ailing you?" He leaned in to get a better look. "Don't get sick on me now, ornery critter."

"He not sick. He just discouraged."

Norbrook nearly jumped, but he hid his surprise. How long had that spooky nigga been watching him? He despised the way some of them could just appear out of thin air. He turned to the young man, who seemed somewhat absent-minded.

"Nigga, did you do something to my horse?"

"Double Sam."

"What?"

"Double Sam. I am."

Norbrook straightened and made himself as big as possible. The young man did not appear to notice. "Did I ask you your name? No. I asked you did you bother my horse."

"Love critters, suh. Wouldn't ever harm 'em."

"You think you're worth more than a horse, boy?"

"I don't suppose."

"What did you say?"

"Naw, suh. Never reckoned so."

"You a simple nigga, ain'tcha?"

"Naw, suh, that be my brotha. Ahm the clever one."

"There's two of ya?"

"Yassuh. Always been. That horse be down for a while. Least till nightfall. I don't just love critters, suh. I knows 'em truly."

Norbrook sighed. "Fix me a pallet, then. Time enough for a drink and a nap."

William

We fled Placid Hall late on a Saturday in October, knowing we wouldn't be missed until early Monday. With a cold snap already threatening, Ransom had insisted that we run before the weather turned for good. Pandora had assured us that Greene would be too sick to leave his slop jar until long after we'd left.

When the time came, we gathered at the Weeping Woman, just outside Placid Hall's farthest edge. Cato, Zander, and I had stood at that tree once before, debating whether the air around it felt freer somehow. The world beyond it was a mystery we were now determined to solve.

Ransom had rounds to make, he said, and he'd be joining us for only part of the trip. He brought us extra clothing to counter the posted descriptions likely to follow our escape. Before stepping foot on the road, I went to have one last meeting with Guinea Jack. I intended to thank him for his kindness and let him know that I was taking Mother and Father Root with me. When I reached his cabin, it was empty and showed no signs of life beyond an over-turned table, a candle stub, remnants of pine knots strewn on the ground, and a pair of broken cups. Cobwebs hung heavy as cur-tains. Where could he have gone? He was too old and feeble to have wandered far, and he could not have been absent long. Someone would have noticed. I saw no footprints around his threshold. I stood in puzzlement, faintly dizzy until I felt a tugging at my sleeve.

"You gave me quite the fright, old man," I said, turning to find Zander looking at me curiously.

"I understand," he said. "Just taking a moment for yourself. I know we're supposed to leave you be at such times, but Margaret and the others were beginning to fret. Who were you calling old man?"

"Guinea Jack, of course."

"Who?"

"Don't pester me, Zander. You know who Guinea Jack is. The old African."

"Are you feeling poorly, William? Unsettled, maybe, because—well, because of our undertaking?"

"I assure you I am steady," I said. "It's simply that Guinea Jack and I haven't been on the best of terms. I was hoping to make peace with him. Foolish of me, perhaps."

"It's not for me to call you foolish, William." Zander looked nervously about the room, as if making sure that I wasn't teasing him. "But you have my word there is no Stolen in these parts with that name."

"Why are you talking nonsense? He lives right here."

"Nobody's been in here for many a harvest, William. Nobody but you."

"Me and Guinea Jack. I have spent many nights with him at that very table, drinking tea from those cups."

"We didn't speculate on what you were doing in here. We just knew enough to leave you alone. Silent Mary would send you biscuits to go with your tea."

"Send *me* biscuits?"

"I used to ask her if I could come sit with you. But she'd shake her head. *Grown folks' business. Stay out.* But she never hinted anything about a Guinea Jack."

"But—"

"William, Margaret will have my hide if we don't show up soon. It's time to go."

I was still deeply confused when Zander and I joined Margaret, Cato, and Pandora at the gathering place. But Ransom's arrival was in itself curious enough to distract me from further thoughts about my missing friend.

He was walking beside Tanner's horse. The paddy roller was riding slowly enough to enable him to easily keep pace. Our worries grew as we watched them approach. Had someone reported our plans? Had Ransom been scheming against us all along? They stopped less than a hundred yards from us before exchanging words we couldn't hear, and the preacher strolled over to join us. Tanner turned his horse around and rode back in the direction from which he'd come.

Ransom's smile as he closed the distance between us did nothing to ease our fears.

"Why did that paddy roller let you go?" I asked. "Is he setting a trap?"

"Surely he will tell others about seeing us here," Cato said, "with no purpose or papers to explain our presence."

Ransom raised his palms and gently patted the air, as if calming a fretful child. "Tanner's a friend," he said. "He means you no harm."

"He's a paddy roller," I said. "Harm is all he does."

"That is what the world needs to think," Ransom said, still smiling. "Consider. He travels the back roads all night, moves along the trails through the woods. He rides with the enemy, knows their thoughts, hears their plans. Then he shares his intelligence with us."

I shook my head. "I can't see him doing all that."

Ransom chuckled. "William, I do believe you have judged that man by the color of his skin."

I thought of the many times Tanner had glared down from his horse while his partner toyed with us. Guinea Jack had mentioned the Thieves' failure to tell us apart from pack animals and rocks. Was I so blind that I could not tell a man from his brothers? It was a notion too heavy to carry. "It's not that," I protested. "It's just that I haven't known of a Thief we—I—could trust."

"You still haven't. Not yet."

Again I sifted my memories of Tanner, half his face hidden under his hat, his hair completely covered. I thought about how little of his features any of us had actually seen, only a sun-roasted patch between his beard and his low-reaching brim. I returned my attention to Ransom. He winked. Then he turned to Little Zander.

"Let's hear it again," he said.

For many nights leading up to our escape, Zander had drawn our planned route in the dirt, a crude tracing that we all tried to commit to memory. Beneath the shadow of the Weeping Woman, Zander recited it one last time.

"The first leg is from here to Lindell Junction, about seventeen miles. The second leg is from Lindell Junction to Murphy's Belt, about fifty miles. The third leg is from Murphy's Belt to Sigourney, about twenty miles, where we will meet a free Stolen who lives by the river."

(Even now I'm leaving out key details, and I don't know if any of us will ever tell the whole story. The fear of disclosing too much remains.)

Ransom explained, again, that because he was a daylight agent he wouldn't be traveling with us. "You might see me at some point in your journey," he said. "You might not. Norbrook will be the one to come after you. He'll be on horseback, of course, and he knows every zigzag and shortcut between here and free soil."

I couldn't help grunting. "Norbrook by himself? There's five of us."

"He's brought back plenty of Stolen, trust. He'll ponder a bit, drink a bit, sleep it off. He drinks more than he thinks, but he's a capable tracker. He'll take his time to make a sport of it."

"How are you so certain what he'll think and do?"

Pandora answered before Ransom could. "We have to know what they think before they know it themselves. It's how we stay alive."

I smiled at her. "What do you mean by alive? You mean sweating and shitting? Might as well be a worm."

"You can sweat and shit at Placid Hall," Ransom said, "or you can do that on free soil. Seems to me there's a mighty difference."

I hadn't heard Ransom use such crude words before. I could tell I was testing his patience, but that didn't concern me. I wanted to make sure he was indeed with us, that there was no betrayal in store.

"Now for the rules," he continued. "Look sharp. Don't let anything—or anyone—surprise you. You need to see things—and people—as they are. You'll have no room for error. Never forget what you're leaving behind."

"And who," Margaret added. She had been silent up to this point. I knew she was thinking of Milton. And Nila. And Sarah, which led me to think of Holtzclaw. I proposed that we make a brief detour and kill him.

"Not a good idea," Ransom said. "Two Forks is in the wrong direction. We made a plan, let's not turn away from it before we've even begun. We have enough risks in front of us without taking on any more."

I heard Ransom talking, but in my mind I saw Sarah sitting on that wagon, waiting for Holtzclaw to drive her back to Two Forks. Margaret had told me about their final conversation and the resigned look on Sarah's face.

"Do you know what he's done?" I asked. "What he does?"

Ransom seemed to expect my questions. "And do you know

how many Holtzclaws there are? Tonight, look up at the stars and count them. For every star, there's a Holtzclaw. He's not our worry right now. Our chief concern is—"

"Getting to free soil," Zander cut in.

"Precisely," Ransom said. "Now, there will be people helping you. Sometimes they'll reveal themselves, but just as often they won't. Assume nothing. Just let them do their work. Their lives are at stake just as much as yours. Open your mouth only when absolutely necessary and talk quietly when you do. Be willing to leave anyone behind. Anyone."

We all nodded grimly, but Ransom was looking straight at me. "Better to lose one than all," he said. "Many an escape has failed because people refused to follow this rule. From Sigourney you'll reach the river. Leave your names right there. You'll need new names for your new lives, so think on that. A man named Char will row you to the other side. Once you're on solid ground, go straight to Seven Bends, a big house overlooking the water. Just follow the lantern. And finally: keep going, no matter what."

These were all instructions we'd heard before, but Ransom had warned us that they were easy to forget in the thick of escape. It wasn't possible to hear them too often. Finally, we backed away into the surrounding oaks, using a piece of brushwood to sweep away the marks our feet had left. The point was not to hinder trackers, Ransom said. Our ancestors once believed that collecting a loved one's last footprints would ensure their safe return. In making sure no one could gather ours, we hoped to never again trudge the haunted grounds of Placid Hall.

"It will look like we took flight," Zander said, "like a band of angels."

Our first hours were unremarkable, although by midnight we were all sleepy and beginning to struggle. It seemed too soon for weariness to stalk us, but already it was creeping into our bones, dulling our senses. Perhaps it came from the recognition of what we'd done, the hugeness of our task weighing us down. We'd spent our lives working under a fierce, punishing sun and resting our sore bodies during nights that were only slightly cooler. Our escape required us to do the opposite, moving swiftly through darkness and resting in whatever shadows we could find when the rest of the world was wide awake. Zander alone showed no signs of exhaustion. He twitched and fidgeted, and often walked so fast that I had to remind him to stick close.

Margaret

After walking for more than four hours, we stumbled into a cornfield for our first brief rest. Crouching beneath a wall of stalks, we shared our food and tended to our feet. I ate little, and what I did eat I ate too fast. We all did, fearful of dawdling too long, but the consequences were different for me. My insides were unsettled.

Ransom had instructed us to stay in the shadows, but few spaces proved more frightening. I saw the pale face of a Thief glaring from behind every tree and peeking between the hay piles in every pasture. Every faint breeze carried their scents of spirits and tobacco. Each twig we stepped on made me imagine the clip-clop of paddy rollers watching the roads. Escaping had been on my mind for such a long time. After I finally made the effort, a sudden, shapeless horror threatened to overcome me. I had warned William against softness, and yet there I was, seized with such a panic that I nearly turned and ran back toward Placid Hall. I didn't want him to see me tremble. I sought a space apart from the others to hide my discomfort.

To calm myself, I recalled a song we often sang in the clearing after Ransom was done preaching.

Yonder

O Canaan, sweet Canaan.
I am bound for the land of Canaan,
I thought I heard them say,
There were lions in the way,
I don't expect to stay
Much longer here.

The words made me feel stronger, though I didn't dare sing them aloud. My resolve lasted only a brief spell, for I soon found myself failing to keep my food down. I looked around for something to wipe my mouth. Pandora appeared, holding a leaf I didn't recognize.

"This will do," she said.

"I suppose it must. Thank you."

She lowered herself to the ground beside me.

"Careful," I said. "I've made a mess."

"I know my way around sick. Is it the baby?"

"No. I think it's just, I'm scared, that's all. Pandora, how did you know?"

She smiled. "I notice things."

"That's true. You do." I smiled back at her. "Are you ever afraid?"

"All the time."

We sat for a while, neither of us speaking, each comforting the other with just her presence. I can't guess the thoughts that occupied Pandora, but mine revolved around my mother, how I had little knowledge of her beyond the hole her absence left in me. In the silence I embraced another liberty that our new venture provided each of us, one that I hadn't thought of before. In addition to going where I wanted and loving whom I chose, I could now claim the freedom to turn a thing over and over in my mind, to consider it from every angle until my examination led me to a certainty. I pondered in this way during our quiet sitting, and in so doing I was reminded of the very resolution that had compelled me to the road. I would know my child. And my child would know me.

Meanwhile, William had been pondering too. After we gathered ourselves and prepared to get moving, he touched my shoulder. I turned to him. Intimate talk was always easier for him under cover of darkness.

"Margaret, what if I had stayed? Would you really have run without me?"

I held his head in my hands and kissed him tenderly. "You know the answer to that," I said.

Cato

We arrived on the outskirts of Lindell Junction early on Sunday, about three hours before sunrise. Ransom's instructions brought us to a bridge across a small creek, where, he said, we would encounter the Dutchman, a man friendly to our cause. We waited under the bridge for an hour until he showed. For his safety and ours I cannot say much beyond his acknowledgment of the signal we offered. He nodded and left us there for another hour before reemerging to lead us to another location. We kept to the margins, through back alleys and away from the main street, although it was empty. Daybreak hovered, threatening to expose us. We made haste to a two-story brick house with a narrow high stoop. The door was ajar, and there was a lighted candle burning on the table. The Dutchman ushered us to the basement, where we were to repose for several hours. Its floor, less forgiving than those in our cabins, was moistened by runoff that had seeped through the foundation. As a consequence, we had to select our sleeping places with care. Ransom had advised us that comfort should be the least of our concerns. We might sleep one night in a cornfield, he said, and the next day in the branches of a tree, or in a hay pile with barn mice for company. He was certainly right about the mice.

Although we remained in the basement for six hours, genuine slumber eluded us. William and I slept with our backs propped against the wall, guarding the rest of our band as they curled on the ground nearby. All of us were fitful, and Zander cried out once, caught in a dream. Pandora shushed him, and he was still again, for a while. I myself had been dreaming of Cannonball Greene's detestable pit. I awoke to sore shoulders as if I had been strapped to his immense wheel, sentenced to a lifetime of trudging in a circle. I wondered if I would be condemned to dream of little besides labor, if I had time enough to learn to dream of much else.

Keeping with his custom, Little Zander was first to rise. By the time Ransom reappeared and roused us, the boy had pronounced his seven and was scampering like a rabbit. Ransom hadn't promised that we'd see him again, and so we greeted the preacher with considerable ardor. He brought us a helping of greasy meat, which we divided while he went upstairs to confer with the Dutchman.

When I reclaimed my makeshift seat beside William to consume my portion, he confided that he, too, had contended with a troubling dream. It involved the strange disappearance of Guinea Jack, an elder he had once revered—a man no one else had seen or known.

"Margaret doesn't believe me," he said. "Zander. No one."

"I have a notion," I told him.

William usually had no tolerance for conjecture. In this instance he was surprisingly patient.

"I'm thinking the man you call Guinea Jack was here before us, in that same place. He lived and died in Placid Hall before we ever stepped foot there."

"An Ancestor. What makes you think that?"

"Before Placid Hall, I knew a Stolen named Isaac, a good man. He died. Every now and again, I see him. He speaks to me. Only to me. He tells me things I need to know, pushes me when I need pushing. How about you? Does your Guinea Jack do that?"

William nodded.

"Then I believe you."

A commotion interrupted us. Zander, having helped himself to a biscuit from Pandora's sack, was just about to bite it when she knocked it from his hands.

"Don't eat that," she said. "Not that one." She picked up the pastry, brushed it off, and carefully rewrapped it in cloth before placing it in her sack. "Silent Mary has a special recipe. Poison. It starts in the stomach. They get the trots, then a fever before dying drenched in sweat. It takes time, but it works."

I thought of Greene nibbling biscuits from a silver tray. Of her standing silently while he chewed.

"Every Stolen cook in the county knows how to make Mary's special recipe," Pandora continued. "They learned how to cook like her at her very elbow, at their Thieves' insistence. The special biscuits are marked with a cross and may prove handy."

"Let's take care with those," William said.

"Yes," Margaret agreed. "In the meantime, let's offer thanks to Mary for her good works. I'm sorry that no one among us knows her recipe."

"In truth," Pandora said, "one of us does."

Again I thought of the silver tray, Pandora's frequent errands to Silent Mary's kitchen. We hardly had time to absorb that intelligence before Ransom and our host clambered down the steps, sharing the burden of a large, unwieldy box. Together, with much clanking and jingling, they opened it and piled the contents on the ground. William and I stood to look as Margaret waved a candle above the pile, illuminating a jumble of chains, shackles, and collars. For a moment we froze as fear and confusion overtook us. Then William leaped.

William

In an instant I overpowered the Dutchman. I held him in front of me, his throat in the crook of my arm. "I knew it!" I said. "You've betrayed us!"

Ransom remained calm. "Oh, William," he said, "if you could but trade a small measure of courage for the tiniest portion of wit. I'm a sinner, it's true. Like any man, I'm prone to moral weakness and capable of endless perversion. But what you accuse me of is beyond my capacity. Pray, have a little faith."

"You're selling us down the river," I said, "but at least one Thief will die in the bargain." I squeezed the Dutchman's windpipe. That the action gave me pleasure was no surprise.

"Preacher," Margaret said. She sounded heartbroken, desperate. "What are you doing? What is happening?"

"Consider, my dear. We don't have numbers. We don't have munitions. To overcome our oppressors we must engage them with an abundance of cunning. They have us outgunned, so we must outthink them. Encourage them to see things as they wish, not as they are."

Ransom picked up a collar and clasped it around his own neck. "To get to the next haven, we'll have to go straight through the heart of town. At its busiest. In broad daylight. It's not what we planned, but new circumstances make it necessary. No one will look askance at a coffle."

None of us moved. I kept our host in my grasp. There was no sound except for his measured, whistling breath.

"Please," Ransom said. He looked directly at me. "Trust."

Cato stepped forward. "I have faith. I don't have much, but I have that." He picked up a collar and put it on.

"You have plenty," Pandora said, joining the coffle.

Little Zander followed suit. "I know what you believe in, William," he said. "You believe in us."

That may have been true, but I still had doubts about Ransom, and I didn't trust our host at all. I couldn't, having so little knowledge of him. Back at Placid Hall, I rarely allowed myself to think much on the likelihood of freedom. I saw such flights of fancy as a form of weakness. When I did think of it, not once did I picture escaping by binding myself in the very instruments I had fled. I was thinking of death as a far more suitable option when Margaret called to me.

"Remember," she said, "we're not meant to die here." Sobbing, she moved to place a collar around her throat.

I released the Dutchman. He fell to the floor on his hands and knees, gasping. "If this is a ruse," I told him, "it will be your last."

Once outside, we trudged with our heads down, avoiding the eyes of Thieves as our ally led us across town. By way of stolen glances I was able to spy a tavern, a dry-goods store, a bootmaker, a silversmith's shop, and sundry enterprises. The clank of our chains joined the neighing of horses and the tap of hammers, the heave-hos of journeymen, the husky chants of laboring Stolen, and the laughter of young Thieves at play, chirpy as birds.

Margaret

We followed Ransom's new plan without running into trouble, finally entering the rear of a strange, weathered church on the far border of town. We caught a glimpse of the surrounding woods before our escort closed the door and freed us from our pretend bondage. Still somewhat uncertain but grateful nonetheless, we offered our thanks. He nodded and departed. The church showed signs of continuous repair. Holes had been patched here and there with splintery planks and even branches that looked freshly torn from trees.

Inside, Ransom gathered us in a circle beneath a ceiling that seemed to be made partly of sky. "I likely won't be seeing you again," he said. "Cato, perhaps you could give us a word?"

Cato cleared his throat. "Ancestors, help us remember," he said. "We come from Strong."

Our heads bowed, we waited for more. But that was all.

"A timely reminder," Ransom said.

I couldn't help crying as I hugged the preacher for the last time. William was last to speak with him before he took leave of us.

"I—I—I," William began, but he could say no more.

"I know," Ransom said. He put his hands on William's shoulders.

Both men nodded. Ransom smiled and left us in the care of our new host, whom I shall call the Deacon.

Tall and soft-spoken, he led us through the sanctuary and into a sort of crawl space that we gained by way of floor planks that he slid aside with practiced care. Because our new shelter was less than waist-high, we had to sit with our backs bent forward for most of our time there. To avoid harming ourselves, we took turns lying on the ground and stretching to our full lengths, the rest of us huddling together to make room. A few pitiful, thin beams of light filtered in through a series of tiny holes in the floorboards over our heads. Hand gestures and whispers took the place of talking, followed by complete silence whenever we heard footsteps or voices, not knowing whether they belonged to friend or foe. We had with us a ration of corn bread and a bucket of water, our only sustenance for many agonizing hours. The thirst was worse than the hunger, as nerves dampened our appetites. The moist heat reduced our clothes to damp scraps. Cramps plagued our sweat-slicked muscles.

For the latter part of our time there, a choir rehearsed in the sanctuary. We heard wailing that we came to understand as voices raised in song, though we could hardly make out the words. Something about spacious firmaments and blue, ethereal skies. There we remained until late Sunday evening.

Before we set out for Murphy's Belt, the Deacon presented us with food and new clothes, including boots. None of the boots fit us exactly, but we were powerfully glad to have them. Although Pandora and I had gone mostly barefoot and so were less accustomed, we were as eager as the others to put them on before we hurried off into the trees behind the church. Our bodies tight from so much hunching and folding, we struggled for some distance before regaining our usual pace. Except for Zander, who showed no signs of ache or weariness.

"I could fly the rest of the way," he boasted, "but don't worry. I'll keep my feet on the ground."

Following the Deacon's instructions, we expected to come upon an abandoned blacksmith's shop where we could shelter for the day. We arrived before sunrise after several hours of stumbling and picking our way through dense woods, including stretches so thick and dark that we held on to each other to avoid losing our bearing. A horseshoe, nailed to the splintery boards above the entrance to the smithy, was the sign we were looking for. The door was ajar, and through the opening we could see a solitary lit candle on a table. William entered first and looked around before beckoning to the rest of us. The air was close and sticky even though there was more space inside than we expected. Besides the remnants of a forge, I saw the ruins of four stalls, each just large enough to contain a horse. Fragments of iron, blackened and tarnished, were strewn on the ground. They kept company with a pair of twisted tongs, broken wooden handles, a busted bellows, and a careless sprinkling of nails. In the dim, flickering light, it was hard to tell if those things had been there for a long time or recently left behind during a hasty departure. The air smelled of rust and ashes, and everything was thick with cobwebs. A grain sack had been left on the ground beneath the table. Inside we found bread and several ears of roasted corn. Three clay pitchers sat on the sill of a boarded-up window, each filled with water.

William, Cato, and I squatted in a half circle. Pandora leaned over the table and pressed her elbows against it as if testing its weight. Zander scooted from one corner of the place to the other, pausing now and again to join our whispered talk. William reminded us that we wouldn't meet up with another Chariot agent until just before midnight. We would have to be still and quiet until then, and carefully ration our provisions.

"A powerful long time, seventeen hours or so, I reckon," Zander said.

"With luck we'll spend much of it sleeping," Cato offered. "Best to try while it's still dark."

Although we were exhausted, it was hard to settle down. Zander, as usual, had the most trouble.

"William," he said, "how about a game of seeds and pits?"

William glared at him. "How about a game of peace and quiet? You see any seeds and pits around here?"

Zander pressed on. "We could use those nails, and maybe some bread crumbs."

"You'd waste bread on a game? You want to play while Norbrook gets ready to ride? Remember Preacher's words," William said. "Cannonball Greene knows we're missing by now."

I sighed. "Do you all realize we'd gone miles and miles and hours and hours without talking about him? About them?"

"That's true," Cato said.

William shook his head. "Not talking about Thieves doesn't make them go away. They're still out there. Everywhere."

I knew that, but he had failed to take my meaning. "Not talking about them, not thinking about them, even for a few moments," I persisted. "Perhaps freedom feels something like that."

"Too soon to talk about freedom," William said. "It has to feel better than a growing stiffness in my bones. Right now, we're just like we were at Placid Hall: at their mercy. No air or food to call our own. We sit when they say sit, go when they say go. Every place we stop could be a trap."

During our talks with Ransom, he had warned against thinking too much about what would happen if we were caught. It would only slow us down, he said. I understood William's frustration, his unease. Running never felt as risky as standing still, when we could hear our heartbeats pounding like raindrops on a roof. But Ransom advised against traveling in the light of day unless we had no other choice.

"No matter," I said, "our bodies demand rest, even if our spirits can't be still."

"Norbrook won't be resting so much," William said.

"He'll pace himself though," Cato said, "out of concern for his horse."

"Curious," Pandora said. "Thieves are careful to avoid exhausting their animals but will work a Stolen to death."

"Pacing or not," William said, "he's coming." He cast a meaningful glance in my direction before moving to take his post near the door. Cato and Pandora found the corner farthest from the rest of us, where they commenced cuddling.

Zander squatted beside me. "Margaret, what do you think is yonder?"

"I don't know. What do you think?"

"I reckon it's the end."

"The end of what? The world?"

"Everything," he said, eyes shining. "The end of everything. You can run. You can jump. You can fall. But you can't just sit there."

"What if it's really like that?"

Zander smiled. "You know, that would be fine. Fine." He stood and began to flip and tumble about the shop, end over end.

"Enough of that foolishness," William said. He allowed Zander a minute to find a spot on the ground before he got up and put out the candle. After the boy finally grew still and the only sounds were crickets and snoring, I found William in the dark.

"You should rest," he said. I snuggled against his chest, burrowing into him until he wrapped me in his arms.

"And you also. I could keep watch."

He chuckled softly. "I have no doubt you could. Perhaps in an hour or two I'll wake you to relieve me."

"We both know that will never happen."

He kissed me gently on the crown of my head. I remained silent, savoring his scent, his warmth, the soft rise and fall of his breath.

"Margaret?"

"Hmm."

"Have you chosen your new name?"

"I have a notion. How about you?"

"I'm thinking on it, but I haven't settled. Tell me yours."

I reached for his hand, laced his fingers in mine. "As you said, it's too soon," I told him. "Not until freedom. Then we tell."

Cato

Our next guide was to come for us in a tarp-covered wagon. One of us would ride up front while he concealed the others among his dry goods and furs and thus conveyed us to Murphy's Belt. The Deacon said we'd know him by the patch over his left eye.

We slept fitfully, as was our custom, then whiled away the remaining daylight according to our individual natures. For me, that meant staying close to Pandora. We had become skilled at expressing affection through smiles and gesture, and even those had often become unnecessary. Proximity was enough. Zander, tired of capturing beetles and bidding them race against each other, had taken to admiring a spider hard at work in the frame of a boarded-up window. He watched so intently that he hadn't noticed William standing beside him.

"A spider is a thief among creatures," William said. "See that beetle on the sill? He's saying his seven. Meanwhile, the spider is setting his trap. Just a-spinning and spinning until the little bug finds himself stolen."

William reached out to pinch the spider between his finger and thumb, but his motion was too casual, too deliberate.

Zander caught his wrist. "Don't!" he said.

"Hush, boy," Pandora whispered. "You're forgetting yourself. You didn't come all this way to give us up with a holler."

Zander held William's wrist until he was sure he would leave the spider unharmed. "All this way," he said. "By Ransom's reckoning, free soil is less than a hundred miles from Placid Hall. A short distance in truth, yet few of us ever get there."

The boy's remarks struck us all dumb. He retreated to one of the stalls, leaving us to wallow in doubt.

By late afternoon, the shadows stretched the length of the smithy and we could no longer discern one another's expressions. By sundown we were parched, famished, and tormented by the prospect of failure. Our resources were dwindling, and our patience had diminished in equal measure. Even later, we became more frustrated when the occasional sounds of humanity had faded and all we heard were our growling stomachs and the ominous baying of distant creatures. Once we were certain midnight had come and gone, our predicament was clear: no help was coming.

Even Zander had lost much of his usual verve. "We should go on our own," he urged. "We can follow the Drinking Gourd. I'll show you."

"The boy makes sense," Pandora said. "There's nothing we can do here but turn to dust and bones."

"Agreed," Margaret said.

She and Pandora gathered themselves and prepared to leave. I rose from the ground, stretched and shook my limbs. William stood in front of the door, arms folded. He turned to me.

"Your thoughts?"

"I have none better."

"Then let's go." He quietly swung open the door.

Margaret stared at William as she moved past him. "Oh," she said, "you think we were waiting on you to decide?"

We crept outside under a sky completely absent of stars.

Zander's knowledge would be useless. No sound or scent provided a hint of the proper direction. We shuffled fearfully in unyielding darkness, holding on to one another, as lost in time as we were in space. The blackness overhead hung low and heavy like something solid; the more we moved the more it descended until we scurried with bent backs, afraid to straighten and bump our heads. Unlike us, sound seemed to move with relative ease. Footfalls, heartbeats, and cracking twigs discouraged us from speaking and thereby adding to the din. We might have traveled for as long as three hours, but in truth I had no notion. I felt turned around, helpless. I feared we were approaching a mesmerizing despair that Ransom had warned us about. He said that Stolen on the run sometimes began to long for all they'd known, no matter how terrible it had been. At least it was a hell they knew.

The ground beneath our feet turned unreliable, threatening to betray us whether we moved or paused. It felt as if we were descending from high ground, down, down toward the center of the earth. Then we were climbing up again, scrambling and struggling to avoid sliding back into a formless void. On we trudged, knowing one another by the rhythm and violence of our breath. Huff. Puff. Stumble. Pause. Stumble. My muscles conspired against me, and my eyes burned from the effort to see.

"The moss," Pandora whispered. "Remember the moss." Ransom had told us it grew on the north side of trees. Timber was sparse around us, but when we touched wood we slid our hands along the trunks. All we found were splinters and loose bark. Pandora sighed, far too loudly for our circumstances. I heard her sink to the ground just behind me. Another exhalation and a soft thump told me that Margaret had joined her. Feeling my way, I lowered myself next to Pandora and wrapped my arm around her. Zander sat next, followed, after a long interval, by William. Too exhausted to speak, we huddled together and fell into an intermittent sleep.

When daybreak approached and our band remained intact, I considered the likelihood that fortune favored us after all. We rose and stretched, except for Zander. He remained low to the ground, squatting on his haunches. To our right, faint pinks and oranges streaked across the sky, now faded to gray.

"The sun is rising over there, so north would be here," William said, pointing. "We've wandered sideways."

"Yes," Margaret agreed, "but exactly how far?"

"Exactly? That's hard to reckon," William replied. "Now that we can see where we're going, we can straighten ourselves out."

"We can also be seen," Margaret said. "Maybe we should find some place to shelter until dark."

William snorted. "There is no shelter anywhere in sight. Sitting still is out of the question."

"But we're worn out," Zander protested, still squatting.

For the boy to admit exhaustion was unusual, if not unheard of. William took no notice.

"Time is wasting," he said, extending a hand to Zander. "We've been worn out before."

The day remained dreary and full of thunder that never led to rain. We made our way through cornfields, sucking dew from leaves and feeding ourselves on stray ears. Unroasted, they were a bother on our stomachs, and we consumed with caution despite our hunger. We passed through country that to some eyes may have seemed beautiful, but I can say without hesitation that its splendor escaped me. Until I set foot on free soil, all land was more godforsaken than blessed, less a pastoral paradise than a hell to endure. During our captivity we often suspected the environment of working against us, not for us. Nature conspired as much as any other force to influence our deprivation.

With sunlight waning, we approached a wood. The copse of

oaks, maples, and poplars suggested a place to hunker down and rest until nightfall. We had a stretch of about two hundred yards where we'd be completely exposed before reaching the tree line. We moved low to the ground, scurrying until we reached the midpoint, when we burst into a ragged trot. Upon entering the woods, we bent from our waists and took in great gulps of air before any of us could speak.

"We come from Strong," Pandora said.

I reached out and took her hand as we proceeded. William and Margaret were immediately behind us, with Zander bringing up the rear. We had gone about thirty paces when Pandora stopped abruptly. William nearly stepped on my heels.

"What?" I asked her. "What is it?"

"Flies."

A sudden delirium of insects enveloped us. They worried our eyes and ears, swarmed our mouths and nostrils. We batted at them furiously, none more than Pandora. She opened her mouth to scream but the flies rushed in. She spat, choking. Shaking violently, she went to her knees and pressed her hands and forehead to the ground. I threw myself upon her until the cloud passed.

Stunned, we brushed ourselves off.

"A puzzlement," Margaret said. "What was that?"

"There," Zander replied.

We followed his pointing finger. The flies streamed toward the body of a Thief slumped in the wreckage of a wagon. A single trail extended beyond the sturdy tree the dead man had crashed against, but its ruts were shallow and must have provided little traction for his wheels. His horses were gone, as were his boots. One blistered toe poked through the hole of a threadbare stocking. A patch sat askew over the remnants of one eye.

"Our escort," I said.

"He must have been on his way to meet us," Margaret said. "We're heading in the right direction."

"Unless he was himself lost," I said. "Besides, we don't know if he was coming from Murphy's Belt."

"He's been stripped of supplies," William said. "Someone's been here before us."

"And they could still be near," Pandora added.

We hushed at once and moved farther into the woods. Under the dense canopy, Pandora and Margaret found a shallow depression a little more than two yards long and just wide enough to hold us if we all lay side by side. We got in it and draped brush over ourselves like a blanket, with William and me at opposite ends. Zander was positioned in the middle between the two women.

"How like a grave this is," he observed, but Pandora quickly shushed him.

Aside from his comment none of us dared even to scratch until we sensed that danger had passed. By then the night was full upon us.

The long stillness had stiffened me beyond any notion of comfort. My muscles rebelled, furious that I was calling upon them yet again without supplying them with proper sustenance. I fought off dizziness as I stood and stretched. I could feel the blood pulsing inside my skull.

William gave no indication of unease, physical or otherwise. He was eager to resume our journey. To his consternation, our women were neither ready nor willing. Still in our hiding place, brush strewn around her, Margaret sat with her hands in her lap. Pandora remained beside her, watching her with concern.

"I can go no farther this night," Margaret said.

"*We* can go no farther," Pandora added. She placed a palm tenderly on Margaret's back.

"We must," William said, glaring at her. "Need I remind you that sitting still—"

"Need *I* remind *you* that I am with child?" Margaret moved her hands to her belly. "Have some consideration."

William softened. "Of course. Forgive me."

"Perhaps," Margaret said. She turned away and looked off into the trees. Her exhaustion spread like a plague, deflating our bodies and spirits. For the moment we were out of arguments, opinions, imagination. We gave her the last of the corn. The rest of us would hold out until the dawn, when dew would reduce our thirst. Until then we struggled to keep our tongues moist and considered the prospect of digging for worms and culling bugs from the underside of rocks. We all understood that we would do what we had to.

When I lay down beside Pandora, she was speaking softly into her clasped hands. "Ancestors, make us thankful," she said.

"Thankful?" I said. "Tonight the word is bitter in my mouth."

"Man, what are you prattling on about?"

"We have no food, no water. No idea where we're heading."

"You have me, right?"

"Yes."

"And I better have you."

"Indeed, you do."

"That's plenty, then. Quit your whining and get some rest."

William woke before me. I spotted him standing a few feet away. His back to me, he was looking down at the ground. I rose and approached him. Soon I saw the focus of his attention: footprints. They weren't ours. Before retiring for the night, William and I had carefully brushed away any signs that might betray our presence.

"A visitor," William said without turning to look at me. "Looks like he stood here a while but withdrew before approaching."

"Norbrook?"

"Perhaps, but he would have left no trace."

"Unless he wanted us to know," I said.

Still stretching and yawning, Pandora and Margaret joined us. Margaret looked better than she did last night, albeit weakened still. Pandora squatted and studied our discovery.

William turned to me. "Wanted us to know what?"

"That he's watching us."

"Then why didn't he just capture us when he had the chance?"

"Because he enjoys the chase," Margaret said.

As we struggled to make sense of this new development, a breeze stirred up and swirled around us, carrying with it a horse's unmistakable whinny.

Zander approached. "Did anyone else hear that?"

Pandora nodded. "We all did," she said.

"We need to run," I said. "Now."

William shook his head. "If it's Norbrook, we can take him."

Margaret was incredulous. "Take him where? It's folly enough to linger near one dead Thief, and now you talk of harming another?"

"We don't even know if it's him," I said. "We don't know who it is. Or how many."

Suddenly, Zander began to giggle. He doubled over, beside himself with merriment.

Pandora put a hand on his shoulder. "Are you all right?"

"I reckon," he said, straightening. "Just thinking about my seven, that's all. I didn't say them this morning."

"This is certainly not the time to think on such things," William objected.

"You would say that, William. As for me, I can't recall the last time I neglected—"

A loud report interrupted him. Zander dropped to his knees. He swayed, then fell on his side. Pandora knelt beside him, but he feebly waved her away. "Better to lose one than all," he said. Blood oozed from underneath him.

Another loud report forced us all to the ground. Bark exploded from a nearby tree, spraying dust and bits of wood. William began to crawl toward Zander, but I grabbed him and held him in place.

"William," I said, "think of your child."

"Zander is someone's child."

He struggled against me but I held fast. "I know," I said. "I know."

Zander's eyes were closed then, his lips moving soundlessly. Saying his seven, I'm certain.

"I'm sorry, Zander!" William said.

"We'll come back for him," he said to me.

I helped William to his feet. Turning, we both saw that Margaret and Pandora were already on the run. In front of us, weaving in and out of the trees.

VIII

Buba
Yali

Well, give me a wig and call me George Washington. Look what I found. A runaway nigga."

Norbrook licked his lips and grinned at Zander. The boy was propped against the overturned wagon, lashed to a wheel. Behind him, the dead driver slumped. Half in the wagon and half out, he rotted in bootless oblivion while flies casually devoured his corpse.

Hands on his hips, Norbrook strutted back and forth in front of a small fire he'd built. "Why'd you go and kill this poor man? Did you intend to take his wagon? I see his supplies are gone. You stole them. You and the others."

His captive said nothing.

"I told Greene you niggas would be easy to track. Hellfire, you left a trail even a sightless man could find. You know how many niggas I've circled and trapped? Neither do I, it's been so many."

"Above it stood seraphim," Zander said, whistling through broken teeth. "Each one had six wings: with twain she covered her face, with twain she covered her feet, and with twain she flew."

Over the course of several hours, Norbrook had punctured, gouged, twisted, burned, and snapped, even collected a keepsake or two in the bargain. There wasn't much of this nigga left. He swung hard, the back of his hand catching Zander's mouth full on.

"Quit the gibberish! Who put you up to this? Who helped you? You will tell me, or I will skin you alive."

Zander spat blood and laughed. "Flying has nothing to do with straining to rise," he said. "Make friends with the wind, wrap your arms around it. It will lift you if you let it."

The boy was a simpleton, capable only of useless babble. His failure to respond in due measure to the torments visited upon him had diminished Norbrook's long-anticipated pleasure. This demented creature was a disappointment, plain and simple. He'd tell Greene that the boy had leaped at him like a raging animal. Fearing for his life, he'd stood his ground and killed him to preserve his own hide.

"Look away, boy."

Defying Norbrook, Zander looked up instead. "Buba Yali," he said.

Norbrook leaned forward and slit the boy's throat. He heard a furious rustling, a disturbance in the trees. He followed Zander's final glance and saw the angel frozen in midair, outside of time. Then the rapid descent.

When Norbrook opened his eyes, the boy was nowhere in sight and he had been strapped to the wheel in his place. Bound and gagged, he blinked as a cowled figure squatted before his fire, turning a sharpened branch in the flames. When it rose and stood over him, he knew at once who it was. Swing Low threw back her hood and he saw the fullness of her lips, the angles of her cheeks, her unavoidable beauty.

While burying Zander, she had seen the marks on his back, the same as her own, and realized that at some point he'd lived on the plantation where she had labored as a child. One day, years before she was born, a Stolen man had refused to work. The Thief in charge, enraged, had ordered him corrected of his rascality through the application of a handful of nail rods, made red-hot through immersion in fire. He took them out and pressed them in the screaming man's back until they had cooled. Afterward he became enamored of the design the rods had left: six circular indentations, in two evenly spaced vertical lines. He ordered the process repeated on all of his Stolen, and what began as a punishment became a well-known symbol of the Thief's wealth and prestige. The family tradition continued into the next generation, with all property born on family land or acquired via trade receiving the mark. Swing Low and the boy shared an entangled history; they might even have been kin.

She had trained herself to remain cool, to never lose her poise or her temper. Even so, she wanted to murder Norbrook slowly, make him suffer like the boy had done. She wanted to give him just enough time to feel the chill of doubt spread through his bones and marrow like an affliction, time enough to wonder if he had spent his entire life with his vision upended, seeing white where there was only black, his imagined birthright of abundance peeled back to reveal a vast pitiless landscape, a cruel deception, a topsy-turvy world.

But she had no time to spare. She removed the branch from the fire. Then she thrust it through Norbrook's eye and upward, until it reached the top of his skull.

IX

Days
Ahead

William

We ran until we couldn't, fearing all the while that paddy rollers on horseback were closing in. Our imaginations turning every sound into the howl of approaching hounds, we pushed on until the ground became soft and moist beneath our boots. Pausing to breathe, we felt our feet sink into welling pools of slime and mud. A few steps farther and the muck was ankle-deep, leading here and there to puddles of dark liquid. Mist rose from each shallow pool, every one of them giving off a sour smell. Behind them, towering trees huddled closely. The moss that we couldn't find earlier seemed to be everywhere, coating trunks and branches. Ferns and shrubs gathered close to the ground.

"Ransom made no mention of a swamp," I said. "When he drew his maps in the dirt, not once did they include this."

"It doesn't matter," Margaret said, "as long as we come out at the right place. There has to be more than one way to get there."

I noticed a makeshift cavern deeper into the swamp, formed by a huge fallen tree. Branches and leaves draped from it to the ground. I pointed it out to the others. "We could camp there," I said, "out of sight. I think I even see some blueberry bushes."

"I am not going in there," Pandora said. She folded her arms across her chest.

Margaret snorted. "Do you have a better idea?"

Pandora pointed to a thin track, barely visible. It wound to the right, avoiding the swamp. "I don't know if it's better," she said, "but we should consider it."

"Wherever we go, we do it together," Cato said to her.

"Yet we left Little Zander behind," I said. I knew the others were thinking of him too.

"There was nothing we could do," Cato said gently. "He was out in the open. Going back would have been too dangerous."

I was not persuaded. "Are we certain of that? He still had breath in him."

"He knew the risks," Margaret said. "He understood. We all do."

"But he was just a boy."

She put her hand on my arm. I wanted to shake it off, but I didn't.

"No," she said. "He was almost a man."

"We can go back and get him," I said.

"No," Cato said. "We cannot."

A thunderous shout boiled up in me. But it had nowhere to go. I turned my back to the others and buried my face in my hands.

"William," Margaret said. She repeated my name, but I didn't respond. She slipped behind me and wrapped her arms around my waist. Gradually the heat in me subsided. I took her hands in mine, and she pressed her cheek against my back.

"I'm sorry to interrupt," Pandora said. "Another pressing question confronts us."

We let go of each other and turned toward her.

Pandora pointed to her ears. "Why has the world gone all quiet?"

We had seen birds and squirrels, we had surprised chipmunks. Once we'd had a staring contest with three raccoons that would have been amusing if we had not been fleeing for our lives. When we interrupted their scavenging they stood and watched us, seemingly without a care, before sauntering off into the brush. Suddenly they were all gone. The chattering and scampering that we had gotten used to had vanished. A vague dread enveloped us like a chill wind.

"It's either the cavern or that track," Cato said. "We have to choose—" He froze, staring beyond us. We all turned to look.

"Ancestors, please," Pandora pleaded, "save us." She stared off into the distance, her face suddenly pale.

I had known about bears since I was a child. Thieves who visited in winter mostly draped themselves in beaver, but now and then a guest would appear wrapped to his neck in bear fur. Shivering in my customary rags, I longed to touch the thick shag, which looked impossibly warm. According to Stolen who labored inside Cannonball Greene's house, a bear's head was mounted on the wall in his study. If not for such knowledge, I might have dismissed the creatures as just another strange notion, no more real than angels.

The bear into whose territory we stumbled was on all fours, breathing heavily. Something about the beast suggested it was as out of sorts as we were. Though it was but a yard in front of us, close enough to charge, I felt calm.

"Back away slowly," I whispered. As we retreated the bear advanced, almost in time with our steps. I looked around, searching for anything I might use as a weapon. Still moving backward, I crouched and dug a stone from the soft earth.

"Don't!" I heard Margaret urge.

Grasping the stone, I turned and stood in a single motion. The bear was now on its hind legs and standing slightly taller than myself. Fur, dense and black, bristled on its shoulders. Yellow claws glistened at the ends of its long arms. It smelled as if it had recently plunged its broad snout into something alive, helpless, and bloody. My first error was looking directly into its small, dull eyes. The second was turning and yelling at Margaret and the others, ordering them to run. The bear slashed at my back, tearing through my shirt and getting a small portion of flesh. I was more angered than hurt at that point, although I may have been too stunned to feel the pain. I spun and with two hands brought the stone down squarely on the bear's snout. My efforts tore Margaret's kerchief from my neck. I felt it flutter loose, and in that moment I knew I was lost.

He responded with a roar, batting at me with the back of his paw as if I was an annoying insect. I fell to the ground beneath a frenzy of claws. I heard Margaret scream. Zander had been the first of our band to fall. I realized I would be next and sorely hoped I would be the last. The bear reared above me. Amid my struggles, I saw an onslaught of arrows, felt them humming inches past my skin. They began to pepper the bear's stout hide, forcing it to defend itself with both paws. Noting its distraction, I expended the last of my strength sliding backward, away from it. To my right, Margaret yelled. She was the last thing I saw, moving swiftly away from me, as if yanked by unseen hands. She fought and yelled before disappearing into the trees. Everything went white.

Pandora

Petrified, I stood and watched as Margaret and Cato ran to William's aid. The brief prayer I offered at first sight of the bear seemed flimsy and desperate when compared to the others' swift action. The flashing claws and bared teeth, slick with moisture, reminded me too much of the ogres and beasts from ever-after tales. Rooted to the spot, I shook my head to clear the fog threatening to overtake me. Through my stupor I saw Cato tackle Margaret, rolling with her out of harm's way. Satisfied that he had subdued her, he stood and crouched as if waiting for the opportune moment to enter the fray. It was only then that I was able to move. I ran and threw myself upon him. He held still, unwilling to drag me near the violence.

"Let me go," he demanded. "He's my brother!"

"And what am I, Cato? What am I?"

"You're my everything."

"Then you mustn't get yourself killed."

He nodded, took my hand, and yelled for Margaret. "Come on!"

"I will not," she replied, rising to her feet. She was shouting and crying at the same time. "I will not leave him!"

I understood Margaret's anguish. What I did not understand

was what she hoped to do or gain. Did she really intend to watch while her man was torn to pieces?

Cato softly spoke my name.

"What is it?"

"I think I hear men. Coming from the swamp."

His words gave me hope. "Knights, perhaps. Just the way the story ends in my ever-after tales," I said. "Soldiers sent by the queen."

He frowned at me. "Paddy rollers, more likely."

Something in his voice returned me to reality. I decided to offer one more appeal.

"Margaret, please," I begged.

"Go!" she said. "Better to lose two than all."

Our eyes met, both of us certain we'd never see the other again. I turned away, and Cato and I tore down the path I had earlier proposed. Behind us we heard the bear's growls, rough and guttural, answered by William's grunts and Margaret's screams. We turned a bend, still skirting the edge of the swamp.

Long fronds stretched across the track. The ground beneath us made thirsty sounds, nearly sucking our boots clear off our feet. The fronds, in response to Cato's relentless pushing, swung whip-like toward me as I hurried behind him. To avoid them I moved with my face toward the ground, as if looking for something I had lost. The noises of hidden creatures returned and gradually faded as our path proceeded away from the swamp. After several hours of our panicked scrambling, the path disappeared and we found ourselves thrashing through woods stretching above firm ground. At length, with our tongues thick in our mouths and our stomachs sour and empty, we saw a blueberry patch. Unable to trust our luck, we hesitated and looked around, fearing a trap set by paddy rollers or a bear lingering just out of sight. Satisfied that we were alone, we pounced upon the fruit. Frantic with hunger, we ate fast and in unadvisable quantities. Once sated, we sat with our backs against the trunks of nearby trees. I had no intention of closing my eyes, but fatigue overcame me. I was asleep for only a few minutes when I woke to the sound of retching.

Cato was a short distance away, bent double and emptying his stomach on the ground.

I tore some leaves from a low-hanging branch and took them to him. "They're dead," he said, dabbing at his mouth. "William and Margaret. And we are stuffing ourselves with berries. The thought of it makes me sick."

I placed my hand in the small of his back. "You don't know for certain," I said.

He didn't seem to hear me. "First Zander," he continued. "He called us a band of angels, remember? Now our two dearest friends."

"I'm as sorry about Little Zander as you are," I said. "As for William and Margaret, they come from Strong just like us. They might make it, Ancestors willing. It's my fault, regardless. William wanted to go toward the cavern, and I refused. If I had said yes, they would be right here with us. It's my burden, and I'll carry it."

"If you had said yes, we would have headed straight into that bear's den. It would have come home and found us there."

I hadn't considered that. "Perhaps," I conceded.

"Not perhaps. For certain. We can argue about this when we get to the other side. We're not just pressing ahead for the two of us now. We're doing it for our friends too. We can't falter." He straightened and rubbed his aching belly with both hands. "Shall we proceed?"

Just before we encountered the bear, a cool, foreboding breeze had reached out and touched us, worrying our hair and annoying our cheeks. As Cato and I did our best to cover our tracks and prepared to continue, I became certain it was gathering strength to blow in our direction again. Nothing seemed more important than staying in front of it.

On two occasions the sound of travelers forced us from our path, now wider and flattened by regular use. The first was a man on horseback who, by his clothing and bearing, suggested a parson. Despite his pale face, the sight of him made me think of Ransom. Where was he then, I wondered as we knelt in the untamed grasses rising nearly chest-high alongside the path. Was he worrying about our ragged band or was he already preoccupied by a new mission? The second involved the procession of a Stolen man and woman, very well dressed, with a young Thief girl between them. They all bore solemn expressions and moved with great purpose, almost marching. The couple walked with heads held high, as if they'd never known the scorn of Thieves or the bite of the lash. If not for the girl's presence, we might have approached and inquired about food or shelter. Instead we waited until long after they passed before resuming our route. Sometimes I dragged Cato, sometimes he dragged me. By the time we tottered to a crossroads marked by a signpost, my feet ached so much they seemed to make noise. Part of me wanted to remove my boots and throw them as far as I could. Another part was reluctant to take them off for fear of what I would see.

"Praise the Ancestors," Cato said. "We've reached Murphy's Belt."

I asked him if he was sure.

"On my seven, I am."

"Praise and thank them indeed," I said. "Ransom told us the worst would be behind us if we made it this far. That means we have about twenty miles between here and free soil. Wait. Cato, how do you know? You read the sign?"

"I did."

"How long have you known your letters?"

He flashed me a quick, embarrassed smile. "Since I was a child."

"You're a man of many riddles, Cato."

"It's a long story."

"I can imagine."

"I know you can. But you don't have to. I'll tell you."

The woods on the outskirts of Murphy's Belt included plum trees, barely twice the height of a grown man, and wild black cherry trees heavy with fruit. The ground beneath them showed signs of deer, but none were around. We were able to scavenge and sup undisturbed. I sat in the cool shade, listening as Cato recounted lessons from a kindly Thief, introduced me to the rules of civility, and told me of the time when, fearing discovery, he chewed up what he'd learned and swallowed it down. Relishing the words tumbling from his mouth, feeling his warmth, enjoying the movements and gestures that were solely his, I pictured years unfolding before me, a future in which we never ran out of stories to share. More than ever I wanted to live a long life full of love and children, ending at last with his voice landing sweetly in my ear. Next to him in the gloaming I felt genuinely at ease, as if we'd outrun any ill winds at our backs. We rested, savoring the stillness until the light faded entirely.

Except for hearthside fires and a smattering of pole-mounted glass globes containing flickering flames, the settlement before us was mostly dark. Preacher Ransom's ally there was a former Stolen man who had purchased his own freedom through his work as a tailor. He could shelter as many as eleven runaways at a time in his cellar. We set out in search of him, determined to keep to the shadows until we came upon a dark face. When we did, we would ask for directions to the tailor's place of business. Our plan was a gamble, we knew. The person we approached might turn us in. Some of our people distrusted freedom, Ransom had told us. Still, others failed to acknowledge the deprived state to which they were confined. Unlike the preacher, I was hesitant to condemn them. Perhaps they relied on fantasy to ease the pain of their predicament, as I often had. I did so not because I was a coward or accepted my captivity. I simply relied on my imagination to get me through the day, which I knew would be exactly like the day that preceded it and the one that would follow. In moments of weakness during our escape, I sometimes felt the comfort of fantasy tempting me again. If not for Cato I might have given in.

We stepped lightly toward the village proper, hopeful that any Stolen who declined to help us would simply move away without attracting attention. So intent were we on finding our people that we failed to notice the bedraggled Thief who appeared suddenly in front of us. His hair was long and stringy, as was his figure. He looked as if he hadn't eaten a solid meal in a long time and had gone unwashed for even longer. Our own appearance likely had similar effect, but we were startled nonetheless.

We struggled to remain calm as the Thief studied us from head to toe, our unease growing the longer he went without speaking. Finally, he settled his gaze on our faces. He seemed to have arrived at a decision.

"You two look like you just fell off a chariot," he said.

Cato and I exchanged glances. In his choice of words, perhaps this stranger was letting us know he was sympathetic to our cause.

"I surmise you could use a friendly hand," he continued.

Cato looked at me once more. I nodded.

"We could, boss," Cato said, smiling. "Much obliged to you, boss."

The man grinned back. Several of his teeth were missing. "The pleasure is mine, most assuredly. Well, come with me. Let's get you where you need to go. I'm called Christian," he said. "Christian Quarles. Who might you be?"

"I'm Greene, boss. This here's Prissy."

"Howdy do." Christian extended his hand, and Cato reached out to grasp it.

"Your kind passes through here often on their way to freedom. It's a pity so many get caught. The miles between here and

Sigourney are thick with catchers. You needn't be concerned, however. My presence at your side will allow you to proceed unmolested. Shall we?" he asked. Without waiting for an answer, he turned and began to walk.

I touched Cato's elbow. "Prissy?"

"Sorry," he whispered.

Quarles moved at a pace that belied his gaunt frame. We scrambled to keep up with him as he darted through narrow passages and ducked underneath windows. He greeted the few townsfolk who crossed our path (all of them Thieves) with a cheery hello and a tip of an imaginary hat. We heard far more people than we saw, chatting and chewing noisily at tables, singing happily to the accompaniment of tuneful instruments, loudly toasting their fellows in a tavern parlor. These last we heard as our escort led us into an enclosure that shared a brick wall with the drinking establishment. Quarles held the door open and waited as Cato and I crossed the threshold. He closed the door behind us and lit an oil lamp hanging from a hook, throwing light into a room larger than its narrow wooden door suggested. It could hold perhaps twenty-five people if they assembled closely. Wide, gray planks, spread unevenly, covered most of the dirt floor. A mound of straw and an overturned bucket occupied a foul-smelling corner. The wall directly facing us was stained with a dark, man-size splotch in its center. Remnants of motley splashes trailed up toward its junction with the ceiling.

Suspicion seized us both at the same moment. We turned to see the Thief pointing a pistol squarely at us. He chuckled. "Prissy and Greene, that's rich. You think I was born in a turnip patch? I know who you are. The two of you ran away from Widow Shockley. She has been looking for you. She's offering a reward, and I aim to claim it."

"I think you may be mistaken," Cato said, raising his palms in surrender.

"What did you say to me?"

"We don't know nuthin' of yo' widder, boss."

"Ha! You don't know nuthin' at all. That's what my pap used to say to me. Don't know nuthin' and won't amount to nuthin'. Looky here, Pa, see what I done? Catched me two runaway niggas. You can go to blazes, Pa."

Finished with confronting his absent father, Quarles waved his pistol as if he was eager to fire it. "Sit," he said to us, "or be shot."

I sat. Cato squatted. "All the way down," Quarles ordered.

Reluctantly, Cato obeyed, relaxing his thighs and lowering his bottom to the ground. "She needs water, boss," he said.

"There's a bucket in the corner."

"That's not for water, boss. She needs food too."

"You will get nothing of the kind."

"Not me. Just her, boss. Please."

"You are mighty concerned with this wench."

"Loves her, boss."

"Love her? Ha! A nigga talking about love. That's a notion."

Since our pairing, Cato and I had rarely depended on speaking to make our feelings known. Long silences that may have caused other couples unease merely strengthened the bond between us. Throughout our escape from Placid Hall we had mostly conveyed thoughts with gestures and nods. During our encounter with Quarles, not even those motions were necessary. All we needed was a glance. When Cato's eyes met mine following his declaration of love, I knew that he was determined to leave that room under his own power or die inside it. He studied his hands for a long moment before looking again at me. He was mere seconds from pitting his strength against the Thief's, and I had no doubt that he would win. But where would that leave us? Discovering that Cato could read had given me yet another reason to admire him. Still, I recognized my familiarity with Thieves, their tendencies and weaknesses, as another kind of learning, and equally valuable. Before Cato could coil his hands into fists, I slowly, noisily, slid the sack of biscuits from the pouch strung beneath my dress. I pretended to fumble with the string that fastened the sack.

"Say," Quarles said. "What you got there?"

"Suh," I said. "If you won't give us any food, please don't eat our biscuits. We is powerful hungry."

"We all have our crosses to bear."

Brandishing the pistol in one hand, he walked over and snatched the sack with the other. He sat against the opposite wall and dumped the biscuits on the floor in front of him. They were dry and hard, but he didn't seem to care. He scooped them up and within seconds was devouring them.

"Please, suh, be merciful," I pleaded. "It's all we got."

Quarles looked me up and down, flour coating his lips and nose. "That ain't all you got. But I shall confine myself to one appetite at a time." He produced a flask from an inner pocket and washed down each bite with a gulp of spirits. Half a dozen biscuits disappeared down his throat, each containing a double helping of Silent Mary's special ingredients. He continued to curse us and his father until his words slurred and he gripped his stomach with both hands, forgetting his pistol.

"Something's happening," he said, his voice full of wonder. "Go to blazes, Pa" were his final words before he slumped over. According to Silent Mary, he would not likely die but would suffer crippling pain and violent bowels for several hours, then be unable to move for several more. By then we would be well on our way to Sigourney.

When we were sure he was out cold, we got to our feet. At the threshold, Cato told me to wait. He ran back and took Quarles's gun. We had no papers, no story to tell if we were caught. I didn't ask Cato what he would do if anyone stopped us. The look in his eyes told me everything. Outside, I leaned on him, and we headed out of the village, staying clear of the lights. A downpour surprised us less than a mile after we began, pelting our heads and shoulders with cold, hard rain.

Margaret

I was wiping William's forehead with a damp cloth when he opened his eyes.

"You stayed," he said.

"I did."

"Why didn't you run?"

I leaned over and kissed him. "You know the answer to that," I replied.

"Where are we? How—?"

"We were rescued. You've been asleep for seven days."

Another two weeks passed before William could walk without help, and yet another two before he was close to full strength. In bits and pieces, I told him about those missing days, among the most remarkable of my life. So remarkable, in fact, that they did much to ward off the terror that made them possible.

As William fought the bear, arrows rained from the swamp, piercing its thick hide until it finally fell. It landed partly on William. Before I could try to pull him free, I was grabbed from behind. I resisted, kicking and throwing elbows, until a hood was draped over my head. I was half dragged, half carried backward, my heels digging a trench in the muck.

My captors took me deep into the swamp and settled me on the ground. When they took off the hood and my eyes got used to the light, I could make out shimmering outlines of a band of ragged people. Men, women, and children were gathered in a half circle, all staring at me. They blended in nearly perfectly with the wetlands surrounding us. One instant I thought I was looking at a man, the next I was sure I saw only a tree. At other times I felt as if I were actually looking *through* these strange, wild people. Lean and tough-looking, some of them carried bows and had quivers of arrows strapped across their backs. A few held either fishing poles or strings of fresh-caught fish. I had concluded that I was perhaps dreaming when a woman stepped forward. She was not young, but she was tall and slender. I felt certain she could leap at me and knock me senseless with a single swipe of her fist. She wore a necklace of bear claws and smoked a white clay pipe.

"Welcome to the People," she said. "I am called Grace."

I would soon learn that the People's territory, completely hidden, was an island perhaps twenty acres across. At its center was a lovely blue lake teeming with fish and fowl. Beyond their border, smaller islands appeared to float in the mist. The People looked very much like William and me, but Grace was quick to point out a difference. "There are no Stolen here," she told me. "We belong only to ourselves. And to each other."

Their cabins were made of juniper, hardwoods, and pine. They placed William in one reserved for the sick, stitched his wounds, and gave me salves to rub into his tormented flesh. I was allowed to sit by him while he slept, but only for brief periods. The rest of the time I was expected to work.

Except for the ill, the very young, and the very old, all the People spent long days at labor. Everyone was trained to handle every task, from nursing and midwifing to trapping, hunting, and cooking. Much energy was devoted to gathering vines and stripping them of thorns, organizing them according to thickness, and passing them along to the weavers. They created baskets, thatch for cabin roofs, and shimmering curtains made for privacy. The People had even sewed simple clothes from vines thinned into thread. The endless, overhanging creepers, unlikely for anyone to get through by foot, horse, or canoe, protected the People from intruders. At the same time, the constant growth threatened to overtake their homes. Each of them wore a long-handled knife strapped to their waist, and a gang of choppers spent each day hacking away at the tendrils that had sprung up overnight. Among them were women much bigger with child than I was, swinging their blades in smooth, powerful strokes. Skilled archers guarded the enclave against panthers and bears.

The food I ate in the swamp remains among the best I have ever enjoyed, although my growing womb, four months' full, may have had something to do with it. During my first meal, I sat next to Grace. At first I thought she placed me there because I was an honored guest. In truth, I realized, it was so that she could observe me closely. Over wild grains, stewed greens, and broiled fish, Grace made it clear that her group valued secrecy above all. She declined my efforts to tell her about our journey and how it led to the edge of the swamp.

"One of our scouts had seen you earlier," she said.

"That accounts for the footprints we saw. Why didn't he cover them up?"

"We left them as a warning. To discourage you from coming near our camp."

"Why? We would have done no harm."

Grace refilled my water cup, pouring from a clay pitcher. "You are strangers," she said. "They always bring harm."

She went on to explain that few stumbled into their society and even fewer were permitted to make their way out.

"But you took us in."

"We witnessed your mate's bravery. We saw him sacrifice himself to save his friends from likely death. He seemed worth our kindness."

Their willingness to share their food, company, and the fruits of their labor made me stronger in ways that I continue to discover. As William's condition improved, I felt more than ready to carry on with our mission. And yet, although I missed Cato and Pandora terribly, I was not particularly eager to leave. One night, while I rubbed ointment into William's rapidly healing cuts, we discussed staying with the People. They liked us, that much was clear. I had proven my willingness to work hard, and they already thought highly of William. He was nearly physically ready to do his part, and I was certain he would quickly stand out as one of their strongest, bravest men. Together we would be useful to any group.

"You are an 'I,'" Grace had told me once. "The People are only 'we.'"

I had begun to reflect on the meaning of *I* versus *we*. How much of Thievery was in me? Could I purge it from me? Was there any way to completely avoid it besides living in a swamp? Could my new experiences enable me to live among the Thieves without becoming too much like them?

Those were questions I would have to ponder somewhere else, not in the hidden society of the People. When I suggested to Grace that we stay longer, she simply said, "You belong Outside." Although she didn't smile, there was kindness in her voice. Still, I knew that she was not going to change her mind.

Early one evening, a young woman of no more than sixteen harvests appeared at our cabin entrance. She wore a necklace of bear claws and was accompanied by five People with bows and arrows. Something about her agile figure and restless energy reminded me of Little Zander. No day had passed without me thinking of him at least once.

"Soon the weather will change," she said. "You are noisy when you move and you leave many tracks. Thieves will find you. It's best you go now, before it's too late. Three of our People will guide you. We hold good thoughts for you and your child."

The guides offered us new pouches filled with food and supplies, but we didn't accept them right away.

"I'm confused," William said.

"As am I," I added. "Where is Grace?"

"I am Grace," the young woman replied.

I reluctantly took a pouch. William did the same. "But the woman with the clay pipe. Where is she?" I asked.

"She is still here. She was Grace. Now I am."

Only then did I perceive that *Grace* was a title that meant leadership, and that no member of the People held it for very long. With her companions, she led us from the cabin to an opening in the trees that we never would have found by ourselves.

"You have not seen us," she instructed. "You do not know us."

Our three guides stepped past us and made ready. We nodded to show we understood. There would be no hugs, no words of thanks, no ceremony at all. We turned to leave.

"Wait," Grace called after us. The two remaining attendants stepped forward and handed us each a long-handled knife. We looked up to thank her, but she was already gone.

Pitfalls aplenty were likely between the People's territory and the place we needed to get to, but Grace's guides could steer us past them. We learned that our route would be much shorter than the course Ransom had planned. They would bypass Murphy's Belt by taking us through the swamp to its far edge before pointing us directly to Sigourney. From there we would be on our own.

Cato

∽

Ransom had shrewdly plotted and planned our escape. Zander had given his life in the middle of nowhere. William stood tall in the path of an angry bear. And what had I done? Despite Ransom's warning, I failed to look sharp and was taken unawares. Worst of all, I put Pandora in danger just as I had imperiled Iris: while the Thief loaded her onto the wagon to take her away, I meekly obeyed as he pointed his gun. Sitting on the ground in that putrid room, watching the tattered Thief smirk at me and leer at the woman I loved, I wrestled with the notion that everything had been in vain.

Furious at myself for committing the same error twice, I swore on my seven that I would make amends. I would atone for the sufferings of my comrades by continuing on the path we'd laid. I would make it to free soil with Pandora by my side. I would father a child someday, raise him up spry and joyful like Zander. I would lift him high enough to kiss the stars. But first I had to kill Christian Quarles.

Staring at my hands, I reminded myself that they were capable of great violence. I would have only seconds to close the distance between Quarles and myself, but I was unconcerned. I would be quick.

Pandora was quicker, and cleverer by far. After we slid silently past the tavern without detection and eventually slipped beyond the perimeter of Murphy's Belt, I thanked her for saving us from a likely death.

"If I have to die, I will die with you," she said, "but it's too soon for that."

The excitement deriving from our narrow escape propelled us for a good while. Five miles or more passed before our soaking bodies reminded us that we needed food and water. Our brisk walking slowed to a painful trudge. We turned our heads to the sky and let the rain fall into our open mouths.

The next five miles took twice as long. Sigourney seemed to move farther away with each step we took. Though our bones and muscles were used to punishment, they found new ways to ache. It was easier to imagine standing on free soil than to conceive of a life free of pain. I pledged to never complain of fatigue or discomfort if we made it out of Thievery alive. My exhaustion and my hurt would be mine alone.

By this time we had become accustomed to the ebb and flow of our determination. We each needed the other to prod or soothe, depending on which action was required to prevent our desperate spirits from flagging. Despite these efforts, Pandora fell to her knees in the middle of the road and declared she could go no farther.

"It's my feet," she explained. They had become so swollen that she could hardly stand.

Murmuring encouragement, I dragged her off the road and into a clump of willows. The sun would rise soon, and we needed to bed down for the day. We dared not remove Pandora's boots in case putting them back on proved impossible. I removed mine and collected more rain. I sat on the ground next to Pandora and invited her to sip. Eyes fluttering weakly, she could barely lift her head. Her voice had subsided to a slight whisper.

"Hold on just a little while longer," I told her.

"Cato," she said, "tell me a story."

"All right. I will tell you about a boy who could fly."

We slept through the entire day and might have slumbered longer if Isaac hadn't shaken me awake. He wore a flat, broad-billed cap of unfamiliar design and a green waistcoat adorned with thin, vertical stripes. A wide, brilliant strip of gold fabric swirled around his throat.

"Follow," he said.

He waited nearby while I roused Pandora and we made our way to our feet. I started in his direction, but he shook his head.

"Not me," he said. "Them."

Isaac pointed. I turned, and again I saw them, the gleaming children, the very procession that had so transformed me during my ordeal at the whipping post. They were not as gray as before, and where faint outlines had once described them, I saw nearly solid flesh. I imagined blood coursing beneath elastic sinews, animating nimble limbs. They marched as purposefully as before. Again I felt the mysterious energy rising from their bodies like mist, and at last I realized the truth about them. Isaac may have been an Ancestor, but those children were not. They did not come before me, and they weren't leaving this world. They were on their way to it. They were the days ahead.

"We need to move," I told Pandora. "Now."

"Why? How do you even know which way to go?"

"Trust me."

I recall few details of the landscape through which we traveled. I do remember feeling revived, my hunger and fatigue fading away as we covered the final miles. Pandora leaned on me for most of these, but my shoulder held her weight with ease. I chanted my seven under my breath as we journeyed, the bright glow of the children illuminating a path that only I could see, all the way to the river at Sigourney.

Our youthful escorts diminished in number until only one was left. She lingered near the doorway of a cabin until we arrived, then faded from my sight. Inside the cabin we met Cole and his wife, Alice, former Stolen who anticipated visitors like us. Their home was not far from the river, where Cole worked as a common laborer. He and Alice were generous souls who fed and entertained us before allowing us to rest until just after midnight. Then Cole led us down to the water's edge. This was not a simple task, as Thieves jealously guarded all the terrain between the town proper and the river. Paddy rollers made rounds all night, and dogs snarled behind every gate, eager to pounce. A skiff or two was sometimes left unattended in hopes of luring and trapping runaway Stolen. Cole was a practiced hand at evading such traps, matched in skill only by Char, the oarsman Ransom had told us about long before. He did little more than nod when Cole brought us forward, never taking his eyes off the water.

We boarded the skiff, but not before Pandora took one last look at the land we'd strived so mightily to escape. Having no desire to do the same, I waited until she was satisfied. Upon Char's advice, we slumped low in case Thieves fired at us from their alcoves along the bank. Unbeknownst to him, I carried Quarles's pistol with us. Firing a weapon was beyond my experience, but I convinced myself I could do it if our circumstances required it. In truth I didn't even know if it was loaded. We worried about Char because he sat so upright that he seemed to invite ambush, but our fears were unfounded. Aside from barking dogs and occasional shouts, we heard few sounds as Seven Bends loomed larger and larger in our vision. The mansion, nearly as big as Cannonball Greene's, sat on a hill dotted with pines. Its balcony was high enough to afford a view of every bend in the river. Candles glowed in the windows, and I could almost feel the warmth of the fire that I was sure was blazing in its hearth. Finally, Char steered us to the dock and wished us well. We saw a lantern bobbing in the air as someone made their way down the slope toward us. I stepped out before helping Pandora ashore.

"Praise the Ancestors," she said, hugging herself tightly.

I thanked Char for his assistance.

"Welcome. Best proceed directly," he said, looking all around. He turned the skiff expertly and pointed it back toward Sigourney.

Pandora and I climbed up to level ground, where we met a man holding a lantern. He looked like a Thief, but I understood that he wasn't. Somehow, I doubted that he answered to "boss" or "suh."

"Call me Abel," he said, as if reading my thoughts. "Abel Godbold. You're on free soil."

Walking ahead of us toward Seven Bends, Godbold said something about food and rest. He hadn't noticed yet that we had paused in our tracks. Pandora and I stood facing each other, hand in hand, our foreheads pressed gently together.

"When we woke this morning, we didn't get to say our seven," I told her.

Saying nothing, she kissed me in response.

"I suppose it can wait," I said. And I kissed her back.

Long months would pass before I learned anything of William and Margaret. Although I feared them dead, I forced myself to fancy them alive and loving, with new identities and a healthy infant. Nearly as much time would pass before Pandora and I learned to sleep soundly in our new home miles from the border. Though no longer Stolen, we depended on the mercy of new acquaintances and feared the lurking presence of fugitive hunters.

Yonder

During that first year of precarious liberty, we gradually settled ourselves enough to mourn Zander properly, as well as remember the friends we left behind. Besides the comfort of memories, we seldom possessed much besides the rags that draped our bones. But, as Pandora had already reminded me, we had each other. That was a beginning. That was enough.

William

When I awoke, Margaret's face was hovering above me. She leaned forward, staring directly into my eyes.

"Your child shall know you," she declared. Then she kissed me. She was more beautiful than I had ever seen her but also somehow changed. Faint creases lined the edges of her eyes and lips. The few locks visible from underneath her kerchief showed a few fine strands of silver. I understood that bearing witness to my recent trials had both wearied and ripened her. This new kind of loveliness was dearly purchased and all my doing. I wasn't sure how to feel about it. Mostly, I decided, I was just grateful.

Margaret told me I'd been asleep for seven days. The bear had slashed my back and dealt a cracking blow to my ribs. I had managed to protect my face with my arms, resulting in deep, jagged cuts running from my elbows to the backs of my hands. "Those scars will just be a story we tell our children," Margaret said. "And don't worry, you are still handsome as ever."

The People were advanced in their healing skills, even more than Silent Mary. They warned me that my bones would alert me to the approach of rain for the rest of my days. In distressful times, they said, it would likely hurt to breathe.

Margaret earned our bread and board—and my medicine—by

the sweat of her brow. When not weaving, laundering, or threshing, she'd come sit on a stool beside my pallet. I sipped from various potions while we lamented our losses and discussed the tasks still ahead of us. Margaret believed that Little Zander had died quickly from his wound, but I was less certain. We agreed that he was likely shot by Norbrook, who since then had been thrown off our trail. Perhaps he dared not enter the swamp, or had been done in by a bear or the People's arrows. Margaret had asked Grace's scouts about Norbrook, but they claimed no knowledge of him.

After five weeks, the People informed us that we'd outstayed our welcome. To our good fortune, they did not bid us leave empty-handed or helpless. Grace appointed three envoys to lead us over miles of swampland toward Sigourney. During the journey, I wondered if the People had rejected us because of me. They had praised me for my courage, but only a few of them had actually witnessed it. Most of our hosts would remember me as a weakling who whiled away the day in feverish slumber—if they remembered me at all. Long days in a cabin reserved for the sick had given me more time to think than I desired. I was steady on my feet again, but some nagging doubts had remained with me. In my mind, I'd fought the bear to save the people I loved, including my unborn child. It should have occurred to me that I would be far less useful dead. What's more, I could have done more harm than good in forcing them to watch me die, and so soon after they'd seen Little Zander fall. Perhaps the People were only being polite when they praised me. Maybe their real feelings were closer to Ransom's. He had once told me that I was both brave and foolish. Did the People see me as a brave man? Or did they consider me a fool, best sent Outside where I would pose no risk? I didn't doubt at all that they regarded Margaret as well fit for their company. She was able-minded, strong, and determined, easily the equal of the best among them. The light inside her brightened the darkness. I resolved to always be worthy of its glow.

Days Ahead

It was nearly dawn when we stepped out of the swamp and proceeded several yards to a scattered pile of branches surrounded by underbrush and muck. Behind this clutter was a dugout stocked with supplies. The friendliest of our guides told us their scouts had established the shelter when exploring the nearby area. We were welcome to remain there until nightfall, when we could easily cover the ten miles to Cole's cabin. Before she left with her comrades, she handed us two documents. "They are freedom papers from Grace," she explained, "in case you are stopped."

I studied mine while Margaret repeated our thanks. The loops and dots had always held my attention whenever I'd managed to glimpse them. Holding them in my hand just then, they seemed to move as if alive. Suddenly I grasped the full meaning of the envoy's words. "Grace can write?" I asked. "She can read?"

"All the People read," she replied. "All the People write." We watched as the three of them turned and approached a wall of thorn-crusted vines. The creepers were packed so densely that the first light of morning could hardly get through. The guides touched them casually, parting the plants like curtains. They stepped through, back into the swamp, and the vines closed behind them.

The People were as skilled at building as they were at everything else. Their cabins were solid yet airy, built to keep out rain, wind, and excessive heat. Inside them were carved tables, chairs, and stools that would likely match those found in any plantation house. While no such comforts were in the dugout, it still showed the marks of thoughtful design. The ceiling, made of thatched fronds, was high enough for me to stand without hurting my neck. Earthen jars of water and nuts were placed in easy reach. Grain sacks and animal skins were neatly stored to use as blankets. There was no room to lie down, but three People, the typical number of their scouting parties, could sit side by side with their legs stretched out before them. Margaret and I rested in this manner after removing our boots and rubbing each other's feet with ointment. She laced her fingers in mine and laid her head on my shoulder. Our shelter was so well concealed that birds and animals fidgeted nearby, unaware of our presence.

Margaret's voice had become a murmur, lulling me to sleep. "Do you think Cato and Pandora made it?" she asked. "Are they on free soil now?"

"I'm telling myself they did. If I say it enough, I will come to believe it."

Margaret raised her head and pretended to stare at me in amazement. "William is confessing belief. I'm sorry no one else is present to hear this."

Her teasing took me back to an argument with Cato. As was his custom, he had been pestering me about what he called matters of the spirit. I had just told him that the idea of heaven made no sense to me.

"And yet you agree that we come from Strong," he'd said. "Tell me, where is Strong?"

I brought Margaret's hand to my lips. "I do believe," I said. "I believe in Cato. I believe in us."

I had far less faith in a mysterious mixture that the first Grace had given to Margaret. She told her to splash it on our bodies before we headed out for Sigourney. It supposedly would disguise our scent to such a degree that paddy rollers and hounds couldn't track us.

"They haven't been wrong about much so far," Margaret said as we prepared to leave that night. She rubbed the greasy substance behind my ears and across my face. It smelled of earth and leaves at first, but it quickly faded, losing its fragrance entirely.

"That is true," I conceded, "but if escape was as simple as applying ointment, every single Stolen would be free by now."

Margaret always had an argument ready. "Not many Stolen have even heard about the People, nor will they."

"Right," I said. "We don't know them. We haven't seen them. Not that anyone would believe our story."

My doubts aside, the ointment seemed to work. At the very least, it caused no harm as we journeyed toward our destination. We stayed off the main road, which was burdened by traffic despite being crooked and cloaked in shadows. Our only hindrance occurred when a wound on my side became unstitched. To stifle the bleeding, Margaret pressed hard against it with a piece of cloth. She distracted me from the pain by telling me about the plants and grasses we'd see if we'd taken our route in daylight, much of the People's knowledge of flora and fauna now secured in her memory. She'd even learned to move as they did, making far less noise than me and leaving fewer tracks. Although stopping now and again to tend my wound slowed our progress, we still made it to Sigourney before morning. A somber Stolen woman directed us to the cabin we sought, but we feared we may have misunderstood her. Uncertain, we hid behind a pair of trees and waited for a sign that we were in the right place. Just when we had begun to despair, a man emerged. Short in stature, he had more fluffy gray hair on his brown face than on his head. He sat in a porch rocker and lit a white clay pipe. After a few puffs, he sighed contentedly.

"It's all right," he said. "You can come out. You're among friends."

Embarrassed, we approached.

"I'm Cole," he said with a smile. "Ancestors willing, your days of hiding are behind you." Cole introduced his wife, Alice, and welcomed us to their neat, spare cabin. Their life was plain and simple, but it seemed to suit them. Alice, also short in stature, was just as good-humored as her husband. The ease with which they made room for us suggested they'd harbored many runaways. They declined to say how many, choosing instead to talk about the days ahead we could look forward to.

"Once you get over, try to see the river in daylight," Cole said after we shared a meal at his table. "Some of the clearest, most beautiful water you'll ever lay eyes on. No rocks anywhere. Less than a mile across. It's a marvel, isn't it, to put so much meaning in such a slender creation. Cross it and you're in another world. A better one."

Margaret asked them why they hadn't moved to free soil. After all, they could go where they wished.

"Most of our kin are on this side," Alice replied. "Little by little, we're getting them over. Then and only then."

I asked Cole how he managed to escort so many runaways through an area infested with paddy rollers and fugitive hunters. Alice remarked that her husband had a way of blending in with his surroundings. That was when I noticed the single bear claw on a leather string around his neck. He had been smoking a white clay pipe, just like the first Grace. Was he one of the People, returned to Outside? I knew better than to ask.

Several hours later, when it was time to leave, Alice packed my wound with herbs and wrapped it with a long strip of clean linen. We bid her a hasty goodbye before we slipped behind the cabin and followed Cole toward the river.

"We'll see you on the other side," Margaret promised her.

When we reached the banks, we discovered that Cole's knack for blending in was just one of his skills. He also knew exactly which constables and paddy rollers would turn a blind eye in exchange for a coin. I told him I would repay him when I could.

"You'll do no such thing," he said. "Our local vigilance society collects funds for that very purpose."

"How can you be sure that those Thieves won't turn around and report you?" Margaret asked.

"I can't," Cole replied, "but it's a chance worth taking."

He pointed out Char in the distance, sitting in his skiff. Cole seemed unconcerned as we approached him, but I felt eyes hidden everywhere in the surrounding trees. I helped Margaret climb aboard while Cole spoke softly with Char. The oarsman nodded, looking straight ahead. After Cole and I shook hands, we gave him our long-handled knives.

"See you on the other side," Margaret repeated.

"In due time," Cole replied.

Char stroked the water with his oars, setting the skiff in motion.

Margaret began to sing softly, barely above a whisper: "'You shall have a little canoe,'" she began, "'and a little bit of a paddle. You shall have a little red mule and a little bitty saddle.'"

"What's that?" I asked.

"Oh, something my mother used to sing to me. I saw this little boat and my mind traveled backward."

Cole had told us that in summer the river was shallow enough to walk cross. By the time we made our crossing, it had risen to about twenty feet deep. Char advised us to sit low, but I wanted to keep my eyes on the banks in case fugitive hunters were skulking in the woods.

"Too dark to see them," Char said. "Most you can do is say your seven. By the time you're finished, we'll be nearly there."

"This would be a fine time to say one's seven," Margaret said, looking curiously at me. "William? How come you don't say your seven?"

"I don't believe in talk. I just do. A fine time to forget that."

"And yet you like to say that it's all in the telling. So tell me, William. There must be a reason."

"I would really like to watch for paddy rollers."

"Why won't you say them?"

"Because there's nothing to say. I was never whispered." I had planned to tell her but had never found the right time. Fleeing for our lives under cover of darkness did not strike me as a suitable moment, yet there we were.

"I was never whispered, and everyone seems to think that means I'm cursed," I continued. "But I'm not. I have you, I have this heart and these two hands. I don't need much else. I don't have seven words. And I don't miss them."

She smiled at me, her eyes moist. "Then you shall have kisses," she said. "Seven kisses every morning, seven kisses every night."

"I will be glad to accept your kisses."

"As well you should be."

Char eased the skiff alongside the dock below Seven Bends. "Best proceed directly," he instructed.

Margaret got out first, then held my elbow as I stepped carefully onto the slippery dock. Char turned his vessel around and quickly pushed off. Above the hill leading to the mansion, I saw a light glimmering. Follow the lantern, Ransom had said. All was quiet, then a shot rang out, fracturing the planks beneath our feet. I pulled Margaret to her knees. My boots lost purchase, and I felt myself sliding off the dock and into the depths.

"William," Margaret shouted, "tell me you can swim!"

"I can!" I replied, paddling helplessly.

I could not. Water rushed into my nose and mouth, stung my eyes. I went down slowly, heavily, as if in a dream. Above me, muffled yelling troubled the water. Blinking desperately, I saw Margaret's arm thrusting down through the surface. I stretched toward her, and she grabbed my hand with both of hers. After a furious pulling, I reached the air. Clambering onto the dock, I flopped on my back. Although I was cold and soaked, my lungs felt ablaze. I sat up, my guts convulsing as I expelled the water I had swallowed. I worried that my heart would burst from my chest, so fierce was its pounding.

"Remember what I said," Margaret reminded me as she removed her kerchief and used it to wipe my eyes. "Your child shall know you."

"I want that so much," I said, still catching my breath. "More than anything." Helping each other stand, we crept toward the bottom of the slope. No more shots rang out, but we remained wary. Our footing steadied as we approached the house. The lantern, swinging in the wind, reappeared in front of us. The man holding it stepped forward.

"I'm Abel Godbold," he said. "Welcome to free soil."

"Thank you, kindly," I said. "We're—"

"I know," he interrupted, noting the scars on my arms. "The man who fought the bear and the woman who wouldn't leave him. I've heard much about you. Please, come." His words told me that he had met our friends. Cato and Pandora had made it after all. Godbold turned toward Seven Bends.

I moved to follow him, but Margaret delayed me.

"Listen," she said, finding my hand. "I have something to tell you."

Lowering my head, I felt her breath on my neck. Then, softly in my ear, she whispered her new name.

Acknowledgments

I would like to thank my Ancestors, especially Iris Bonner Harris and Rebecca Knox. Because of them, I am. I'm also grateful for thoughtful guidance and kind support from my editor, Dawn Davis, and my agent, Joy Harris. I was fortunate to receive able assistance from Jordan Cromwell, JennyMae Kho, Diva Anwari, Livia Meneghin, Spencer Johnson, Emily Paramore, Prerna Somani, Angela Siew, and Shaylin Hogan. This book would not exist if not for the loving encouragement of my wife, Liana E. Asim, and the five Wonders of the World: Joseph, G'Ra, Indigo, Jelani, and Gyasi. I am forever obliged.